Possession and Politics
Part One

By

Melanie Munton

Possession and Politics, Part One

Copyright © 2015 Melanie Munton

All rights reserved

Cover Design by Damonza at

www.damonza.com

Print Edition

No part of this publication may be reproduced or transmitted in any form or by any means, electronic or mechanical, including photography, recording, or any information storage and retrieval system without the prior written consent from the publisher and author, except in the instance of quotes for reviews. No part of this book may be uploaded without the permission of the author, nor be otherwise circulated in any form of binding or cover other than that in which it is originally published.

The author acknowledges the trademarked status and trademark owners of various products referenced in this work of fiction, which have been used without permission. The publication/use of these trademarks is not authorized, associated with, or sponsored by the trademark owners.

This is a work of fiction and any similarities to persons, living or dead, or places, actual events or locales is purely coincidental. The characters and names are products of the author's imagination and used fictitiously.

TABLE OF CONTENTS

PROLOGUE
CHAPTER ONE
CHAPTER TWO
CHAPTER THREE
CHAPTER FOUR
CHAPTER FIVE
CHAPTER SIX
CHAPTER SEVEN
CHAPTER EIGHT
CHAPTER NINE
CHAPTER TEN
CHAPTER ELEVEN
CHAPTER TWELVE
CHAPTER THIRTEEN
CHAPTER FOURTEEN
A LETTER FROM THE AUTHOR
ACKNOWLEDGEMENTS
ABOUT THE AUTHOR

"There is an invisible strength within us; when it recognizes two opposing objects of desire, it grows stronger."

Rumi

PROLOGUE

Gwen

Maybe this isn't such a good idea.

I nervously twisted my hands in my lap and watched the bright city lights flash by the window in a kaleidoscope of colors and blazing fluorescence as the cab driver weaved in and out of D.C. traffic. My heart was pounding at a dangerously fast pace and I could feel perspiration begin to gather on my forehead. I tapped my foot impatiently against the floor of the cab as my conflicted emotions warred an intense battle in my head.

Can I actually go through with this?

Is this the kind of person I am?

What if someone finds out?

I seriously considered telling the driver to turn around, but before I could utter a sound, he slowed to a stop in front of my destination. Staring out of the window at all the people walking by—people who could possibly recognize me—I wondered if I should still tell him to take off. Not giving me much time to contemplate it, the driver announced the fare in an annoyed voice, breaking me out of my thought process and forcing me to make a decision. I dug some cash out of my purse, handed it to the disgruntled man, and tentatively stepped out of the cab onto the sidewalk.

Looking up at the hotel, a new wave of apprehension settled over me and caused my pulse to spike again, for what was probably the eight hundredth time since I stepped into that cab earlier. Every ounce of my self-preservation was screaming at me to turn back around, call another cab, go home, and forget that any of this ever happened. I didn't have to put myself through this level of stress. I didn't have to do any of it.

But I wanted to.

Although I wasn't being forced to do this, every fiber of my being, every cell in my body, was telling me that I actually *did* have to. The notion that I had any choice in this particular matter went out the window weeks ago, which brought me to this moment. The decision I made here, on this sidewalk, in the next few minutes could very well change the course of my life.

But you knew that already didn't you? That's why you came here, for a change. For something more.

If I was being honest with myself, I made the decision as soon as I stepped into that cab, or possibly even before that. Maybe whenever I put on this dress. Or maybe it was weeks ago when I felt something inside me shift. Who really knew when it happened, but the point was, I had to make a move right now. Gathering up all the courage I could muster and taking a deep breath, I held my head up, steeled my shoulders, and walked through the hotel doors.

A slight sense of alarm slammed through me as I walked through the lobby towards the elevators. Anyone could have recognized me as I stood out on that sidewalk, foolishly staring up at the hotel. *Anyone could recognize me in this lobby too, for that matter.* Keeping my head down and my pace brisk, I made my way to the elevators and pushed the "up" button with more force than was probably necessary.

Please, don't let anyone see me. Please.

It wasn't like politicians or their families were celebrities, but we did get noticed in public, and there were always stories—oftentimes fabricated but not always entirely false stories—about our personal lives. That is, if you were interesting enough. The more boring you were, the more the press tended to leave you alone.

Well, this would definitely garner their attention.

After what felt like an hour, the elevator finally arrived and to my absolute relief, no one was inside and no one else seemed to be waiting for a lift. So, I stepped inside and pressed the button for the eleventh floor.

Looking at my reflection in the metal doors, I ran my fingers through my long, blonde waves and situated them over my shoulders. Checking my makeup wouldn't do much good since my reflection in the doors was blurry at best but I still went through the motions of clearing out any excess lipstick at the corners of my mouth and smoothing out the skin underneath my eyes, ensuring that my mascara hadn't smudged.

I untied my trench coat and straightened out the black dress I wore underneath. The coat wasn't necessary in the June heat, but I thought it could help me look a little less conspicuous. The dress was form-fitted, hitting just above the knees, with thin, spaghetti straps that crossed in the back. It showed off every inch of my curves in a flattering and classy way, rather than in a trashy, "lady of the night" kind of way.

For possibly the first time ever, I allowed myself to really appreciate the fact that I looked good in something other than pearls and cardigans. I felt sexy and confident, like I could do pretty much anything I wanted to in that moment and it was, quite frankly, addicting. I wanted to bottle this moment up and savor it because, based on my past experiences, I knew it wouldn't last. *It never does.*

Although, as I looked at myself in the doors, with my black pumps, trench coat, and styled hair, I realized I probably *did* look like a lady of the night and my behavior really wouldn't suggest otherwise. A lone, scantily clad woman, lurking around a hotel and sneaking up to a room at this hour of the night and in this city? I had to laugh at the irony of the situation. It surely was not the first time that a man of power and influence in this city had a secret rendezvous with a woman in a hotel room for the night. Though this particular situation was much more complicated than that and I could just imagine the headlines if it were to be leaked to the media.

Don't think about that now. You promised yourself that you would have one night of losing yourself in the moment. One night of uninhibited pleasure. The real world will be there waiting for you tomorrow, so for this one night, pretend nothing else exists.

Shaking myself from any pessimistic thoughts, I concentrated on what was about to happen. Nervous apprehension was quickly replaced by lustful desire as I thought of the person I was going to meet. Memories of the past several weeks and hopeful longing for the evening's events entwined in my head as a deep ache coiled in my belly, causing enough heat to travel throughout my body that even my fingers and toes tingled with anticipation.

This is what I want. This is what I need.

I was so lost in my daydreams, I didn't hear the ding of the elevator and didn't even realize it had stopped until the doors opened in front of me.

This is it. You can do this.

Recalling the room number I was given, I turned right and walked to the very end of the hallway, stopping in front of the ivory-colored door that had the gold numbers of the room engraved across it, shining like a beacon to me. Everything in the hallway was calm and quiet, a complete contrast to the flourish of noise and activity that was taking place inside my head. I was doing my best to relax but with little success. My breathing was erratic from both fear and excitement. My heart was beating so fast I thought it might burst from my chest. And my legs were beginning to tremble so bad I wasn't sure if I would even make it inside the room.

You have to calm down. Deep breaths.

As I was sucking in oxygen and shaking out my hand to stop the trembling, I raised my arm and knocked on the door.

Everything is going to be okay.

A few seconds later, the door opened and I looked up into the same blue eyes that had been front and center of my dreams for the past month and a half. In that moment, when I could finally look my fill without the paranoia that usually followed, when I could smell what had most recently become my favorite scent in the entire world, and when I could stand in his presence with total and utter abandon, everything calmed. My thoughts quieted, my breathing steadied, and peace overwhelmed my senses almost immediately.

It felt right.

This felt right.

Somehow, despite the tribulations that surrounded our attraction to each other, I knew that this was where I belonged. I couldn't explain it and hadn't been able to since the beginning, but this was different than anything else I'd experienced before. And I was done trying to ignore it. The universe was trying to tell me something and, by God, I was going to start paying attention.

Maybe this was finally my happiness, staring me in the face.

Or could this be my ultimate despair?

No, don't think like that. Not tonight. Not now.

The man standing in front of me met my eyes with that burning gaze he always had for me—those piercing eyes that had mesmerized me since I first saw him—and his mouth spread into one of the sexiest, most breathtaking grins I had ever seen in my life.

"Hi, Gwen," he said in a deep husk of a voice that was so characteristically *him*. That sound alone, those two words spoken in that voice by *him*, ignited the fire that had slowly been building inside me to a full-blown flare-up of hunger and need. I could barely say the next words to him.

"Hey, Clay."

He opened the door wider so I could walk past, not once losing eye contact with me to peruse my body even though I had left the trench coat open and my long legs were on full display. Without any hesitation, I walked through with my eyes locked on his as he quietly shut the door behind me. With that action, he had effectively shut out the rest of the world. From this moment forward, my life would change.

I would change.

Nothing would ever be the same again.

CHAPTER ONE

THE HEROINE AND HER DRAGON

Gwen

Six weeks earlier
May

"Gwen! We need to leave in five minutes!" William yelled up at me from downstairs.

"Alright, I'll be right down!" I shouted back, tamping down my irritation. I never liked being told what to do, but one would think that I'd be used to it after all the years of demands, commands, and "requests" that had been barked in my face.

I looked at my reflection in the mirror of the marble-top vanity in the master bathroom. I smoothed back my blonde hair to ensure every piece was nestled perfectly into the stiff chignon at the base of my neck. I doused it in hairspray so that it would remain impervious to all forms of weather throughout the night.

Not that I much cared. But William undoubtedly would, as would my mother, who we were meeting for dinner along with my father.

My makeup was applied with careful precision so as not to appear overdone and tacky but also not light enough to give me an unkempt look. These words and this ritual had been drilled into me from an early age—an age that was probably considered too young to start wearing makeup by some parents' standards—by my mother, who constantly demanded perfection and, above all, obedience.

I quickly touched up my pale pink lipstick and fastened my pearl necklace and matching earrings, then inspected my ensemble for the evening. The dusty rose sleeveless blouse highlighted my lipstick in a soft, elegant way. The blouse was tucked into a cream pencil skirt and I finished off the look with a pair of slingback nude heels, which my mother would probably consider "too high" but I didn't care. I preferred wearing heels that gave me a little extra height and showed off my legs. If that made me a "harlot", so be it.

I thought that perhaps the light colors were a little too harsh on my pale skin, but I didn't have time to change. I grabbed my cardigan just in case I got chilly in the restaurant and rushed to the closet to grab a clutch off the shelf, throwing the essentials inside at rapid speed: a small mirror, lip gloss, breath mints, a couple of Advil, and my ID. I didn't really need the ID but I always took it with me anyway, and I pretty much always needed the Advil.

I took the steps downstairs quickly but gingerly in the heels and headed toward the study to announce that I was ready to go.

And there he was. My fiancé, William Callahan, sat in his leather wingback chair, looking relaxed with one ankle resting casually over his knee. But the furious way his fingers flew over the keypad on his Blackberry—and the way his brow was creased in concentration—would suggest that he was anything but.

Not that this was anything new. I recognized the calm and almost demure façade he put on in and *for* the public, even though I knew inside he was like a powder keg waiting for a release. I didn't know what I would do if I ever did see him completely at ease. It just wasn't his nature.

He wore a pinstriped gray suit—he loved his pinstripes—with a white shirt and a black and white paisley tie. His dress socks were black and his black dress shoes were so shiny that I was pretty sure I could see my reflection in them. His hair was a chocolate brown with some graying at the temples, cut short and parted off-center, always combed and styled with not but a hair out of place.

He was a fairly large man, with broad shoulders and a tall six foot two frame, which towered over my five foot four petite build. He'd started to gain some weight in his midsection, mostly from all the beer, whiskey, scotch, and brandy that he was constantly pouring down his throat. At thirty-seven, he was ten years my senior and it was starting to show.

Nevertheless, he was still a daunting man, who often used his size and physical strength as an effective tool of intimidation.

Everything about his look screamed power and class. He certainly was powerful, but classy? Not by my definition. I didn't think that word should ever be used to describe the man who sat before me, nor would anyone else if they knew the actual meaning of the word and certainly not if they knew him like I did.

He seemed to sense my presence then and his head shot up in my direction, instantly locking his eyes with mine. Those eyes unnerved me more than anything else about him. They were so dark most of the time that their natural color was hardly ever discernable. Although they were supposed to be a dark brown to match his hair color, they were normally black. A cold and lifeless black that reminded me of a shark's, a fitting comparison for his demeanor and personality.

Over the time that we'd been together, the color of those eyes had become almost a warning to me, like a mood ring. The darker his eyes were, the worse he was. They were black when he was stressed, they were black when he was angry, and they were black when he was turned on. Unfortunately, those were the three emotions I saw most often emanating from those eyes, at least around me. I did my best to stay away from him when they were as black as a moonless night, but I wasn't always so lucky.

I loathed the very sight of this man.

He pasted on a tight, fake smile and asked, "Are you ready?"

"Yes. Shall we go?"

Prim, polite, and obedient. That was how he preferred me, and I struggled with it on a daily basis. I thought that after a couple years of dating it would get easier to bite my tongue and keep from lashing out at him the same way he did me, but it didn't. It never got easier and it never got any better.

"Yes, the car's waiting," he replied, standing up and slipping his phone into his jacket pocket. He put his hand on the small of my back and led me to the front door, holding the door open for me as I crossed the threshold.

With any other man, his touch and gesture would seem gentlemanly, affectionate even. But I knew better. These actions weren't derived from any kind of love or tenderness he felt towards me but were instead manufactured out of possession and control. The complete and total control that he maintained over me and every other aspect of his life. He expected this and more and accepted nothing less.

Our driver Roberto, an old but sweet Italian man, smiled at us while holding open the door to the black town car. "Good evening Mr. Callahan. Miss McKindry."

"Hello, Roberto. How are you this evening?" I asked with genuine affection in my voice.

Roberto had been my parents' driver since I was a little girl and I'd known him for as long as I could remember. He was always kind to me and I had always sort of thought of him as my adopted grandfather.

"Very well, thank you," he replied without losing his smile and closed the door after we were seated inside.

The trip to Adriano's, the restaurant where we were meeting my parents, passed in general silence. William was once again enthralled in his Blackberry, while I stared out the window, watching the city of Washington D.C. pass me by.

Though I tried to stray from the direction my thoughts were taking me, I couldn't help but wonder, once again, how my life ended up here. How I was so helpless and lacked almost all control of my own life. Then again, I'd never had control of my own life. Not really.

From an early age, obligation and duty had been the invisible hands forcing me into my appointed role. I was, after all, the daughter of one of the most respected United States senators in the country and of one of the most prominent socialites in D.C. society. I was expected to act as such. Period.

Everything in my life, all my life, had been chosen for me. My schools, my friends, my activities, and even my hobbies were part of a carefully constructed persona that my parents never once allowed me to stray from. If I defied them, I was punished, harshly, even at the age of twenty-seven. My father ruled with an iron fist—sometimes literally—and my mother domineered with menace.

I had once been rebellious and free-spirited at heart, which had only served to tighten the hold that my parents had wielded over me from a young age. They did everything they could to break me down into nothing more than a meek girl, operating under blind obedience and quiet composure. Unfortunately, I had to admit that it had worked, for the most part.

They used my fears against me and subdued me, conforming me into the image of what the daughter, and only child, of a US senator and renowned socialite should look like. They told me that this was how one had to act in our world. If I screwed up, the backlash our family would suffer could have repercussions for years down the road. Their futures rested on my shoulders as much as it did theirs. I was ashamed to admit that they terrified me then and they terrified me now.

But now that fear had duplicated and multiplied because there was more pressure on me now than ever. Now, there was someone who I feared more than my parents and he was sitting right next to me. I slept beside him every night.

William Callahan was selected by my parents as my future husband over three years ago, but the engagement had to be announced at the right time. The right time in William's career as well as my father's. There was no proposal because there had been no choice for me. There was simply a decision between William and my parents of when to make the announcement and I read the article in the newspaper the next day.

That was it. It was the perfect union and I had no say in the matter. William's family had all of the right connections for my father and vice versa. The Callahans were basically a household name in D.C.—everyone knew them and everyone wanted the perks of being associated with them. So despite the age difference, and the fact that it was a veritable arranged marriage, the two men struck up an agreement. I found out about the arrangement during a conversation in which my parents listed all of William's qualities and the finer points of what an "advantageous marriage" it would be. Then they encouraged me, none too pointedly, that it would be a very good idea to date the man.

An advantageous marriage? What is this, *Pride and Prejudice?* Who talks like that anymore? I protested all I could but it was no use. We had our first date the following week and the rest was history. My parents reminded me at every turn that it was my duty, my responsibility to "uphold the family name," and I would not refuse or there would be consequences.

I knew the kind of man William was before I even met him and that was why I couldn't say no. If my parents didn't make me pay cruelly enough if I refused him, William certainly would. He was not a man to be rejected or dismissed. From the moment he and my father shook hands and sealed the deal, I knew I was locked in and there was no escaping.

The only stipulation that William had was that I moved in with him as soon as he proposed. My parents, of course, didn't like that and thought that it might attract some bad press, but he wasn't going to have it any other way.

At first, I stupidly assumed he wanted it that way because he wanted me close and that he might actually care for me. It didn't take me long to figure out that I was way off base. He wanted me nearby, yes, but in order to monitor my actions and keep track of me at all times. It was all about the control he had when I was nearby, and his possessive nature would never allow me to be too far away. So, I moved in right after he gave me the ring.

Not exactly the stuff fairytales are made of.

I thought about running away many times throughout my life, about leaving everything I knew behind and starting somewhere new. But then I woke up and realized that could never be my reality. My parents would make sure that I would have nothing if I ever tried to leave, and I wouldn't put it past my father to use physical force.

Now that I was bound to William, I had no illusions that I could escape this life. Whatever my parents would do if I left, William would do much worse. He thought of me as his and only his. His property, his possession. He didn't take kindly to his possessions leaving him or being taken from him. He saw it as a direct attack on his pride and ego and he never allowed it to happen. Sometimes I felt like I was living in sixteenth-century England, being victim of an arranged marriage to a man I didn't love. I might as well be locked in a tower, guarded by a fire-breathing dragon.

Only I knew my story wouldn't end with a knight in shining armor coming to rescue me. That kind of thing only happened in the books.

Bottom line: he would never let me go and I knew it.

With my parents, I fought to keep myself, to maintain who I was deep down inside and not let my mind and soul become poisoned. With William, it was harder to do. I was never good enough, always inferior to him, yet I had to please him. Every day, I could feel his venom spreading throughout my body, corrupting my mind, but I tried to remain resilient. Why, I didn't know because nothing would change. I would forever be trapped in this stagnant, loveless purgatory, struggling with dreamy notions of freedom and individuality. I knew how ironic it was to be so enmeshed in the inner workings of America's government—with its leaders, who work solely for the purpose of protecting the people's rights—yet one of their own was denied the one thing this country guaranteed to all of its inhabitants: freedom.

I was an American, yet such a concept was so foreign to me.

For now, however, I was going to endure because I had no other options. I still had thoughts of escaping and finding happiness away from this life someday, but I had to be smart about it and I needed time to plan. I had to keep those positive thoughts hidden somewhere in the recesses of my mind, otherwise I wouldn't survive. I wouldn't be able to get through every day if I thought this was how it would be for the rest of my life.

I believed in God and I believed that he had a reason for everything he did. I hadn't yet figured out the reason why I was in the current situation

I was—or why my whole life had been the suffocating bubble that it was, for that matter—but I had to trust that there was a purpose for it all and that the end result would be worth the suffering.

So, I would be the perfect little fiancé and daughter until the time was right to leave this hell behind.

We arrived at the restaurant and William got out first, holding out his hand for me with that phony smile plastered on his face. Ever the respectable politician.

What a joke.

He led me to the entrance with a tight grip on my elbow that appeared as if he were simply being protective of his fiancé. *Yeah, right.* He was always like that in public: extra controlling, very possessive, and extremely territorial. It was like he was daring anyone to challenge his authority, ensuring that everyone around knew that I was his property and he was the only one allowed to touch. And there wasn't really much I could do about it.

We were led by the maître d' to a secluded area in the back—reserved for the most special of patrons—where my parents sat at a corner booth and stood up to greet us with hugs and kisses when we arrived at the table. *Aren't we just the cutest little family?*

Before we all sat down, my mom gave me an obvious once over, most likely to approve or disapprove of my outfit. She did this every time she saw me, usually followed with some sort of comment of either praise or disdain. I was twenty-seven years old and my mother still thought that she had to inspect everything I wore.

Can we serve the wine now and leave an extra bottle for me, please? I silently pleaded with the waiter.

"You look lovely," she commented with a tight smile. I was momentarily shocked at her words. That was the nicest compliment she'd given me in *years.* Apparently, I passed inspection. *Rare but I'll take it.*

"Thank you, mother. You do as well."

She really was a beautiful woman but her cold detachment and veneer of stoicism made Marcia McKindry look years older than she was. It was like the woman had some sort of aversion to any feelings that in any way resembled love or affection, like she was allergic to it. I knew very little of her life before she married my father, and I had no idea what happened in her past to make her act the way she did. But I was somehow convinced that she hadn't always been like this.

"Hello, dear," my father said as he leaned over to kiss me on the cheek.

"Hi, Dad." We all took our seats and my father immediately ordered a bottle of wine for the table and scotch for him and William.

Like William, my father was a very intense man, and like my mother, he didn't often show any affection to her or to me. He had always been very career-oriented and was rarely around when I was growing up. Power and control meant everything to him and nothing was ever too far beyond his reach. He had ruthless ambitions and a reputation for having a fierce, cutthroat approach in business and all his pursuits.

I supposed the reason he pushed William at me—or pushed me at William—was because he saw himself in my fiancé and trusted him to represent the McKindry name well.

The two men immediately started to discuss business while I was stuck hashing out wedding plans with my mother.

"I've almost completed the guest list and then we'll have to get started on the seating arrangements right away. If we're expecting over three hundred people, then we'll need to be very meticulous on where everyone is placed."

My mother kept going on about the most important people invited and where they belonged and who belonged next to them, but I didn't care. If I had my way, it would be a small ceremony with just close family and a few friends, rather than the extravagant affair that she was planning. Marcia McKindry, however, would never allow such a thing so it didn't matter to me who she invited. As long as I didn't have to mess with it, she could do whatever she wanted. It wasn't as if I was excited about the whole ordeal, anyway.

"I think it was wise to postpone the date until after the election. There's a lot more availability at all of the venues after that first week of November," she said as she picked through her salad the waiter had just brought.

William was running for Mayor of Washington, D.C., and it was now the height of the campaign season. The whole summer was going to be filled with political rallies and debates, social appearances, and charity events that we would both be attending. He preferred that the wedding be postponed until after the election so he could focus all of his attention on the campaign, so he told reporters. It was really because he wanted the media spotlight to be solely on him while he was campaigning. Then after he won, he could focus on his role as the doting fiancé/husband and family man.

Again, I didn't care if I was the target of media attention or not. In fact, I preferred not to be but that was impossible with having the last name McKindry. Even though the wedding planning had become my own personal hell, the longer I could postpone becoming legally bound to the man sitting next to me, the happier I would be.

Not that the situation was anything to be happy about because it really wasn't. Instead of being happy like I should be when planning my wedding, I just felt...*empty*. Empty and numb.

For the next hour, I blankly stared down at my plate, barely touching my food, nodding to my mother's comments and responding when appropriate, though I'm not even sure what I said. When mother got up to use the bathroom towards the end of the meal, I turned my focus to my father and William's conversation. Anything to distract myself from thinking about linen colors and the types of appetizers we should serve at the reception.

"I'm sure Clay Masterson will put up a hell of a fight. I was acquainted with his father back when he was in office and the man fought tooth and nail for every piece of legislation he passed through," my father said matter-of-factly, as he held his glass of scotch out in front of him, absently swirling the amber liquid as he spoke.

William gave an inelegant scoff and replied, "I'm not worried. He's running as an independent and when was the last time anyone but a Democrat won this election? Plus, he's young and doesn't have enough experience in any kind of office to establish the credit he needs to even make this a race."

William was always arrogant enough to think that his background and family name were enough to allow him to win the seat in any office he ran for.

"I wouldn't bet on it," my father retorted, "Sam may not be in office anymore, but the Mastersons are still well-liked in the community and they've got a lot of connections. I'm just saying be prepared for a few surprises."

William drained the rest of his drink without replying, seeming completely unconcerned. I didn't know much about William's opponent, Clay Masterson, but I was secretly hoping that the man gave William a serious run for his money.

CHAPTER TWO

THE HERO AND HIS ARMOR

Clay

I anxiously twiddled the pen around in my hand and tapped it against my desk, a habit I'd had since I was kid. I wasn't OCD and didn't have a tic, but sometimes I just felt better when my hands had something to focus on rather than sitting and being idle. Or, perhaps it was more because it allowed my mind to have something inane to concentrate on rather than what it was *supposed* to be concentrating on.

In this case, I was supposed to be focusing on my assistant, David, and his exhaustive recounting of my schedule for the upcoming week. I was absorbing everything David was saying, responding when prompted, but was really only giving him about fifty percent of my attention. It wasn't that I was trying to be rude or that I didn't care about my responsibilities; I just wished sometimes that this job was a little more simplistic than reality allowed for.

After all, running for Mayor of Washington, D.C. wasn't exactly a one-dimensional enterprise. There were so many behind-the-scenes aspects to an undertaking like this, it was easy at times for someone in my position to forget the end goal, the overall purpose. I'd known that going into this, though, and truth be told, I wouldn't change anything. Sure, I would love to change certain facets of my everyday goings-on, but that was the world of public policy. There was always progress to be had, and that's what I loved about what I did. I wanted to affect change in a big way and see the betterment that would hopefully follow it.

I realized that I probably sounded like I was blowing smoke like any other politician, but I was sincere. What some might consider to be "lofty ideas" were in fact the foundation of my principles, the basis for all of my career goals. I genuinely cared for my community and the hard-working individuals in it, the reasons behind which were deeply engrained in me and were seated as far back in my childhood as I could remember. I reflected on those reasons whenever I felt like I was losing sight of my objectives or allowing someone else's agenda to cloud my judgment.

The next several months would be a testament to that judgment and said principles and I was ready to tackle everything head-on, at full force. Everything I had worked for my entire life had been building up to this moment, this election, and I wouldn't allow anything, or anyone, to stand in my way.

I could actually remember the first time I'd realized that I wanted to go into public service. I'd been eight years old, walking the streets of D.C. with my father after one of my little league games. We'd been enjoying the summer afternoon together, stopping at a park to feed the ducks swimming in the pond and buying ice cream cones from a street vendor.

As we were walking down the sidewalk eating our ice cream, we passed by a homeless gentleman sitting against the side of a building. His clothes had been filthy and ratty, his shoulder-length hair looked like it hadn't been washed in years, and he was giving off a foul, putrid smell that indicated he'd probably been sitting there for days.

But as an ignorant eight-year-old, I was curious rather than disgusted. I asked my father why the man was sitting on the ground and why he was so dirty. He responded because he had nowhere to live and I'd been…flabbergasted, for lack of a better word. I could remember feeling completely astounded that the man had nowhere to go at night, no bed to sleep in, no place to take a bath or brush his teeth. And where did he eat his dinner? I remember saying all of this to my father and couldn't believe that he hadn't been as outraged as I was about the situation. My best friend Parker didn't have a lot of money, I knew. His clothes didn't always fit and they weren't always clean, but at least he had a home to go to at night. At least he had a family. Well, I hadn't ever seen his parents but I knew he had brothers.

As we got closer to the man, I could see that he had a cardboard sign in his hands. I could read pretty well by that point, even for an eight-year-old, and could easily read the scribbled black letters that said:

NO MONEY FOR FOOD. HUNGRY

I honestly hadn't understood at the time why the man didn't have any money. I remember thinking, *didn't he have a job? Where did all of his money go?* It was such a strange concept to me, being hungry and homeless, and I, at my young age, didn't want to accept that it was part of the real world. I'd looked down at the ice cream cone in my hands and realized that the snack wasn't even a meal to me. It was a treat that my father was kind enough to buy me because he could afford it and wanted to make me happy. I'd already eaten lunch before my game, and I knew Mom would have dinner ready for us by the time we got home. I had all of that and this man had nothing. Just a cardboard sign.

What I did next I did without hesitation and without a word to my father.

I took the ten dollar bill my mother had given me that morning for whatever I wanted at the game and ran back to the ice cream vendor. I didn't know what flavor to get, so I just got my favorite and ran back to the man. I bent down in front of him and held out the ice cream cone, his head raising at the action. "It's mint chocolate chip," I said because I really didn't know what else to say to him.

He looked at me as if I'd spoken German but slowly extended his hands to tentatively take the cone. He made a couple noises in his throat like he was trying to speak and was eventually able to get out, "Th-thank y-you."

Then I dug the change the vendor had given me out of my pocket and held it out to him. He looked up at me again, but his eyes were glistening this time, like he might cry. "You keep it," I said.

Again, he looked lost for words but he accepted the money as a tear escaped out of the corner of his eye. He met my eyes and whispered with what I now realized was a stammer, "Th-thank you v-very m-m-much."

I beamed a huge smile at him. "You're welcome," I responded. When I walked back over to my dad and looked up at him, I could see that he had tears in his eyes too, and I wondered why everyone around me was suddenly crying.

He put his arm around my shoulder, hugging me into his side and said, "I'm proud of you, son." I still didn't understand why he seemed upset, but I was happy that he was proud of me for whatever reason.

I could remember that day like it was yesterday. After that, I'd asked my dad hundreds of questions about poor people and how we could help them because I was determined that we could. We could help them turn their lives around and get them off the streets. I smiled to myself, thinking about what a tenacious, if not aggravating, eight-year-old I must have been.

And ever since then, I've wanted to help other people in any way that I could. As I got older, I realized that the best way to do this was by having the power to initiate the change I so desperately sought. This power would best come from holding a public office, thus beginning my political career.

And I wouldn't have it any other way.

Lately, though, something had been feeling off. I couldn't really put my finger on it, but my mind was drifting off more than usual and I was questioning myself more than normal. Not questioning my career decisions necessarily, but questioning the course of my life in general, I suppose.

My career was where I wanted it to be right now—well, if I won the election it would be—but that was pretty much all that there was in my life at the moment. I wasn't dating anyone and hadn't officially dated anyone in over a year, which sounded like a long time, but I just didn't have time for a relationship. I had to devote all of my time this summer to this campaign, and it just didn't make sense to get involved with anyone.

In fact, it was that very reason that my last relationship ended. Well, for the most part. Kelly and I dated for almost two years and it had been the most serious relationship I'd ever had. She'd been starting her career in journalism when we met and I'd been working at City Hall. We met at a charity event and immediately hit things off, discussing everything from politics to sports to favorite vacation spots. A few dates later and we were an official couple.

We went strong for about a year and a half, developing an easy routine between her irregular work hours and my commitments with various organizations and committees. But the last six months of our relationship had been rocky, at best. She'd become too distracted with work, and I'd been getting frustrated that we didn't spend enough time together. It had started to feel more like we were work associates, rather than a couple. We started fighting constantly and hardly saw each other at the end, so I eventually ended it. She didn't make a big fuss over it because she knew that we didn't have a future together, so we parted ways on good terms.

Looking back at it, I don't really think that I was ever in love with Kelly. Although I cared for her deeply and still do—I wish her the best and want her to be happy in life—I just never felt that spark with her. Sure, I'd been attracted to her on a physical level, the woman was beautiful. And we had plenty of things in common on an intellectual level and had a lot of similar goals. But I hadn't been head over heels, need to be around her 24/7, takes my breath away when I see her, in love with her. And I'm positive she hadn't felt that way about me either. We just fell into a sort of familiar rapport and created a bond that had worked so well for us that we hadn't even realized when it had started to transform into something else. We thought we had something that we didn't.

But that was okay because I know now that she wasn't the girl for me. We hadn't ever discussed marriage or children, which was another sign to me that we definitely weren't supposed to end up together. I don't have any regrets, though, because I learned a lot about myself during that relationship and I wouldn't change anything. I think it was just part of the course of my life that led me to where I was at now.

I'd make time to find the right girl someday, get married, and start a family whenever the rest of my life settled down a little and I found some stability. But no woman had tempted me to even consider it yet, not even Kelly. In some ways, yes, I was a bit of a control freak. I liked order in my life, and I liked to do things a little bit at a time so I wasn't completely overwhelmed.

I had a plan. A plan of how and when I was going to accomplish everything that I wanted to in my life.

What I didn't realize at the time was that life didn't exactly care about your plan. Life had a plan of its own and it didn't care if that plan messed yours up to shit.

❦

"Yeah, Dad. I'll be there in about five," I said through my phone. I listened to his response and gave a quick "okay, bye" before I hung up and tossed the device in my front seat. If I had my way, I would turn the thing off for the rest of the night and enjoy the peaceful silence, but I'd never hear the end of it from David if I did. Suffering through the incessant phone calls and texts that I would no doubt be receiving from him and some of my other colleagues was the lesser of two evils.

I had the windows down on my Scion FR-S as I drove through the suburbs on the outskirts of the D.C. city limits, headed for my parents' house. Dusk was settling on the city, creating a brilliant confection of oranges and pinks that reminded me of cotton candy at the fair. I breathed in the smells of barbecue, freshly cut grass, and a smell that just said *summer was here*. This was my favorite time of year. There was just something about the beginning of summer that made everything feel so exciting, like the beginning of a new adventure. Since I was a kid, every summer began for me like a precipice to something big, making me feel like anything could happen in those three months of total freedom.

With campaign season upon us, though, those three months were going to be all work and no play. The schedules from here on out would be insane, I would have almost no free time, and forget having a social life. I was attacking this campaign at full-speed and we were going to be giving it everything we had.

This might all sound miserable to some, but strangely enough, I loved it. To me, this was the most exciting thing of all and I couldn't deny that I strongly felt like something major was about to happen in my life. I didn't want to jinx myself, but I had the sense that things were about to change.

Whether that change would be good or bad, remained to be seen.

A few minutes later, I pulled into the driveway of my parents' modest Dutch colonial and could already smell my father's famous steaks on the grill in the backyard. My parents were wealthy but they never flaunted it and I always appreciated that about them. They could certainly afford to live in a larger house in a more upscale D.C. district, but they loved their neighborhood, and the house had been big enough for our family over the years so they saw no reason to move. I was fine with that because this house felt like home.

I loved that every time I walked through the doors I was guaranteed to be greeted by my mother's cinnamon candles and my father grunting and groaning as he worked on his newest house "project", whatever it may be at the time. I loved that my mom always had a welcoming smile on her face when she saw me and a warm hug to give. And I loved that no matter how many years went by, the house always felt the same every time I visited, like no time had passed at all. It didn't matter how long my sister Kinley and I had been away, things didn't change. We could joke around the same way, play the same games, and act like the same family we were when I was a kid.

Not everybody could say they had a great childhood and an even better family who always supported them and stood by them. I was very fortunate that way and yes, I knew it, especially since my best friend Parker hadn't been as lucky.

I walked through the front door and there it was, cinnamon. Cinnamon and barbecue and just like that, I was instantly relaxed. Within ten seconds, my mom came bounding in from the kitchen with her American flag apron on—the one she always wore when cooking—and the biggest smile on her face as she wrapped me up in a hug.

The woman had been a doctor for over twenty-five years with long and irregular hours, but she had always made time for her family. She'd come home exhausted from pulling a double shift but had somehow found the energy to make dinner for all of us, wash the dishes, and do the laundry before she went to sleep, all accomplished with an unbelievable cheery disposition. I liked to tease her that she was a witch with some kind of magical powers because she was simply an unstoppable force of nature. She liked to call it her "mom magic," and I couldn't argue. She definitely had it in abundance.

In my book, Diane Masterson was a saint.

"Hey, sweetie," she crooned in my ear, "how are you?"

She stood back and appraised me, like only a mother could. You know, to see if I've lost weight from too much stress or have bags under my eyes from lack of sleep when I've been working myself too hard. She had a unique way of chastising you that made you love her even more because you knew she was only saying it because she cared so much.

"I'm good, Mom," I smiled at her. "I've been eating my vegetables and getting a good seven hours of sleep a night." *Most of the time.* I may have fudged the details a little but she didn't need to worry.

"Now don't you be smart with your mother, young man. Nobody said you have to have dessert, you know." She slapped me playfully on the arm as she turned back towards the kitchen with me following closely behind.

"Please tell me it's what I think it is," I pleaded. *Please let it be her chocolate sheet cake!*

"What do you think?" she asked over her shoulder.

Thank God. I swear that cake had healing properties. It was so good that you just had to eat one bite and all of your problems would melt away—except for maybe an expanding waistline, but it was more than worth it.

"I knew deep down you loved me," I joked as I opened the refrigerator and pulled out a beer.

"Most of the time," she retorted, never missing a beat.

"Dad out back?" I asked, heading for the door that led to the backyard patio.

"Yes, he is. Complaining about needing to redo the entire deck because the wood is getting too old and rickety. Please talk him out of it before he starts pulling out the boards himself. He still hasn't figured out that *he's* the old and rickety one, not the wood."

I laughed. "You know that's never stopped him before. That man will be hammering away at something when he's ninety." And he would. My father always had to have something to do. Drove my mom crazy but that's what made him even more lovable.

"Not if I put him in a home," she said flatly, but I knew she was joking.

"He'd break out of there within two hours. We both know it."

She sighed dramatically as she stirred the fried potatoes she was making. "Yeah, I know. God bless him."

She smiled to herself as she said it. She loved that man more than words could describe and he felt the same for her. It was an admirable, lasting love they had together. It was the kind that all romance novels were based on and the kind that everyone should be jealous of. I knew I was and I constantly wondered if that kind of love was in the cards for me, if I would ever be that lucky. I'd love to eventually have my own home like this with its own characteristic smells and sounds, with a wife and kids to share it with.

Jesus, where is this coming from? What was going on with me lately? Why the hell was I thinking about marriage and children when I wasn't even dating anyone? The stress must be getting to me more than I thought. I opened the beer bottle and chugged half of it in two gulps, hoping it would clear my head of such ridiculous thoughts.

I walked out the back door and sure enough there was Dad, squatting down and examining the boards of the deck with his toolbox sitting not too far away. A dangerous combination.

"You're going to hurt your back squatting like that if you're not careful, old man," I jested. Sam Masterson hated being called old or having his strength or virility questioned. It was entertaining to goad him and he took the bait every time.

"I've never had a bad back a day in my life. Old man, my ass," he muttered more to himself than to me but I still smiled.

I walked over to the grill to inspect the steaks that smelled amazing. They looked even better, mouthwatering. If my mom had "mom magic", then my dad had "the grill gift." He could take anything ordinary, put it on the grill, and practically transform it into five-star cuisine.

"Steaks will be done in ten," he announced, reaching for his hammer from the toolbox.

"Perfect. I'm starved." I plopped myself down on a lounger and put my feet up. *Oh, that felt good.*

"How are things at the office?" he asked.

He was a former Virginia State Representative, so he knew what it took to make it in the political world. He had loved his time in it, but had been relieved when it was over. He had always supported my decision to go the same route, but he never overstepped his boundaries by getting too involved. Without me even needing to say it, he understood that I needed to do this on my own and make a name for myself without his influence.

"Going well. Been busy, of course. David's got a million things lined up and I've got a good feeling. We'll just take it day-by-day, though, and see how things go."

"Heard much from Callahan's camp?" he asked. He stood up slowly, loosening his stiff joints while trying to hide his obvious discomfort. *Never had a bad back a day in his life.* I tried to hide my smile as he walked over to check on the steaks, apparently abandoning his deck deconstruction for the time being.

"Not much right now, but supposedly he'll be focusing a lot on tax reformation and reallocating city budget expenditures during the campaign, which I think is a bold move."

William Callahan was my toughest competitor for the vote into the mayoral office. I hadn't met him yet, but he was reportedly an aggressive and clever adversary, who often took on tough issues with a no-holds-barred approach. I'd heard that he'd made a lot of enemies over the years due to his reputation for being arrogant and having a short temper. That notwithstanding, voters viewed him as someone who could get things done, and regardless of how I personally felt about the man, he was going to be a formidable opponent.

"It's apparently his nature. He likes to go for the public's jugular and is supposedly fierce in his debates, too, but can shoot himself in the foot if his attitude gets in the way." My dad took a drink of his own beer as he started to transfer the steaks to a pan to take inside.

"Yeah, we were working on strategy today and how we're going to handle that." I trusted David and my advisors implicitly when it came to strategy, but there had been some heated moments at the table this afternoon because of some differences in opinion. It didn't happen often but this was also a big election—the one we'd been working for—so there was certainly more pressure and the stakes were higher.

"Just remember to stick to your guns. Show the public who *you* are, not the guy who's trying to beat William Callahan. Do you understand what I mean, son?" he asked in a hard voice. It wasn't harsh, just firm.

"Yes, sir," I answered because I did understand. From the beginning of my political career, he'd told me to not lose sight of who I was and what my goals were. He didn't want me to get swept up in other people's objectives but to maintain my own course and achieve what I set out to accomplish. I wasn't about to forget that.

He nodded his head, satisfied. "Good. Let's go inside before your mother thinks I've killed myself tearing up the deck."

I stood up and followed him to the door. "Nah, she's learned over the years not to freak out unless it's taken you too long to come back inside for more beer. Then she worries."

I jumped out of the way, laughing, before he could slap the back of my head. He had a smile on his face as he walked past me into the kitchen.

An hour later, Mom and I were sitting at the table eating chocolate cake and drinking coffee while Dad washed the dishes. They always had that routine. If she cooked, then he cleaned up and vice versa. I was happily stuffed with the first home-cooked meal I'd had probably since the last time I'd come over for dinner. I didn't exactly have a lot of time to cook at my apartment.

"Have you guys heard from Kinley lately?" My younger sister was now a freelance photographer in New York City. She moved there after going to college at Brown and was apparently loving the city and her job. We'd always had a strong relationship over the years, but I hadn't spoken with her in a couple of weeks, which made me feel like a jerk. I needed to make more time to talk to her.

"She called me a couple of days ago to say she was going to Costa Rica next week for a photo shoot. She sounded excited," my mom said, her voice sounding a little deflated. She was happy that Kinley had apparently found her niche in New York, as we all were, but I knew she missed her daughter and wished she was a little closer to home.

"Is she seeing anyone?" I asked. Not that I really wanted to know, but she wouldn't tell me if she was, and I couldn't help but be protective of my little sister. I just wanted to make sure she wasn't dating an asshole.

"Not that I know of, but you know her. She wouldn't tell any of us if she were," my mom replied, sounding slightly irritated.

It was no secret that Kinley was a private person, even with her own family. Though, she hadn't always been. In fact, she had had a very open, bubbly personality when she was younger, which changed when she got to college. She had become more introverted and reserved, almost shrinking inside herself. Although a lot of that could have just been from growing up and experiencing the real world—because let's face it, it's not always a nice place—but I'd always suspected it was more than that. Something specific that she didn't want to share with anyone, and I didn't want to intrude by asking. I assumed that it may have had to do with a guy. The fact that she never brought guys home and didn't seem to date much at all was probably not a coincidence, but it wasn't my business. After all, other than Kelly I never brought girls home. Kinley had still made something of herself and seemed happy so I wasn't about to make a big deal of whatever changes she was going through.

"Don't sound so miffed, Di," my father chided softly, "she'll let us know when she finds the right guy. You should be happy that she's being so picky."

"I know, and I am. I just worry about her. There's a difference between being picky and just being indifferent," she said as she played with the locket around her neck, while staring down at her coffee mug. The crease in her forehead was evidence of how concerned she had become for her daughter.

I put my hand over the one on her mug. "She'll be fine, Mom. She's just finding herself in a new city with a new life. She's strong and smart. You don't need to worry so much."

She gave me a genuine smile and patted my hand with her other one. "I know, honey. Both of my babies turned out pretty good. I think I'll take credit for that."

My dad let out a sarcastic grunt from the sink. "Woman, they would have walked all over you if I hadn't been around. You're too sweet for your own good."

Mom's smile turned mischievous at his comment. "Yes, dear. Your status as 'man of the house' has never been in question." Then, she leaned toward me and said in an almost whisper, "But we know who's really in charge." She leaned back and winked at me and I couldn't contain my soft chuckle.

Dad didn't seem to hear that last bit. "Well, at least I can say that both of my kids know how to swing a hammer, thanks to me," he said, sounding proud of himself.

Mom looked at me and rolled her eyes.

I just shook my head and smiled at both of my parents.

Yes, I was very fortunate indeed.

CHAPTER THREE

STARS AND STRIPES

Gwen

Where is that server with the tray of champagne? I needed a refill and I needed it twenty minutes ago.

My eyes scanned the expansive ballroom, but all I saw were servers with trays of hors d'oeuvres. *What does a girl have to do to get a little alcohol around here?* Not that I was a big drinker, I really wasn't. I usually stuck with wine or champagne at events like this, but this night was making me wish that I had something a lot stronger tucked away somewhere because tonight may never end.

Tonight was the Stars and Stripes Club dinner, an event hosted by a social organization that existed solely for this dinner, and an event that William had to attend as a mayoral candidate. And being his fiancé, he was expected to bring me along. Let's just say, I was ready to leave before I even stepped foot through the door.

The type of crowd that was here tonight lacked in variety, needless to say. Only politicians, city officials, and other prominent members of D.C. society were invited. Basically, it gave all of them the opportunity to mingle together in the same room at the same time and get drunk in an acceptable social setting. This, of course, meant that I was well acquainted with almost every individual in the room, which made for a somewhat dull and unremarkable evening and an atmosphere that was anything but comfortable.

It made me almost regret wasting this dress on an event such as this. For some reason, I had been in the mood to put in an extra effort with my look tonight. I wanted to try something a little different, so I'd dug in the back of my closet and came out with a dress that still had the tags on and decided to be bold. I'd bought the dress one day when I was feeling particularly daring, but I hadn't had the nerve to wear it before tonight. It was a floor-length silk gown in a gorgeous scarlet red that made me think of a rose in full bloom. It had a deep scoop back that showed off more skin than my mother probably would have deemed appropriate, and a slit going up my left leg that stopped just above the knee that I *know* she would not have approved of.

But I didn't care. It was surprisingly comfortable and I felt beautiful in it, so I was going to soak up that rare feeling for as long as possible. I'd been a little nervous about William's reaction. It was entirely possible that he wouldn't have approved and would make me change. Fortunately, though, he didn't say a word—not even a nice word about how I looked but I didn't exactly expect that either. He just assessed me for a few minutes longer than normal and then walked away to grab his phone before we headed out the door.

I had been relieved because I felt confident in this dress and I needed a little bit of that right about now.

William had kept me by his side for the first hour or so that we were here as he made the rounds and ensured that the crowd saw us together as the "happy bride and groom-to-be," and then ditched me as soon as everyone got the message. I was mostly ignored by the men in the room because they typically only wanted to "talk shop" amongst each other, and I would apparently bring nothing of value to the table. I had grown up in this environment my entire life and was now engaged to a Callahan, but everyone still assumed that I didn't know what I was talking about when it came to public policy.

The women were almost as bad, drawing me into conversation after conversation about the wedding and how the planning was going, as if I had nothing else going on in my life that was worth discussing. I guess to these people I probably didn't, but I could only describe my ideas for the floral centerpieces so many times before I either lost my mind or the contents of my stomach.

Hence the desperation for massive alcohol consumption. Not that I could get drunk at an event like this—both William and my parents would filet me alive—but I just wanted enough to ease some of the tension.

There were really only two good things about tonight: 1) my parents weren't able to attend because my father had some business come up in New York City at the last minute, and 2) there was a chocolate fountain. End of story.

So, I loaded my plate up with strawberries, bathed them under the confection of chocolatey goodness—one that would have made even Willy Wonka swoon—finally found another glass of champagne, and prepared myself to endure more of the same, mind-numbingly droning gossip and chit-chat of the supercilious social scene that was my future.

And all I really had to look forward to right now was more champagne and chocolate.

I guess it could be worse.

❧

"...But that's why it's important to have variety in what's offered. What's the point in having an imagination if everyone is reading the same thing all the time? After all, 'it's in literature that the concrete outlook of humanity receives its expression.' All human expression deserves to be shared through written word," I finished and took a sip, or gulp, of champagne.

I was really starting to get frustrated with this conversation and annoyed with the company. These women were narrow-minded bigots and had no appreciation for freedom in literary themes, arguing that certain subjects—such as erotica and some taboo-themed topics, along with really anything written by right wing enthusiasts—shouldn't be allowed to be published. And I was about to lose my temper and make a fool of myself, if I hadn't already. Unfortunately, the buzz from the champagne wasn't helping to calm my nerves.

"I couldn't agree more," came a deep, husky voice behind me.

I turned and came face-to-face with a stunningly striking display of male embodiment. *Wow.* My heart rate spiked as soon as I locked eyes with his bright blue ones and my mouth suddenly became dry despite having just downed half my glass of champagne.

He flashed a dazzling smile when I still hadn't said anything, which only made everything worse. His teeth were white and perfectly straight and the dimples on both sides of his cheeks only made him more painfully attractive. His hair was black and cut short with barely enough of it to grab on to.

I tried to stop my eyes from roaming up and down his beautiful tall body but couldn't. He had to have been at least six foot four and looked to be very sturdily built. I could see muscles under his broad shoulders but they didn't look horribly bulky. His skin was tanned which only made his teeth look even whiter and overall, made his face even more delicious.

He had on a black tux that looked custom-made to his body as every inch of it fit him to perfection. He stood with his hands in his pockets, seeming completely relaxed and in his element in this room full of high-ranking government officials and financial moguls. Well, casual he may be but this man exuded confidence, power, and sex in the most scrumptious package.

I could see all of this with just one look and he'd only spoken four words to me.

Who the hell is this, and how had I not noticed him sooner?

"Alfred North Whitehead, am I correct?" the gorgeous tux-clad stranger asked, shocking me.

"Um…" I couldn't seem to articulate any words. I could barely form coherent thoughts in my head, let alone vocalize any. *He knows who I had quoted?* I cleared my throat and tried again. "You know Alfred North Whitehead?" I hated that my voice sounded so shaky.

Pull yourself together, Gwen. He's just a man. A very beautiful man who you can't even touch, so get rid of the dirty fantasies fogging your brain.

He put a hand over his chest, acting pained. "You wound me. Should I be insulted that you think I'm not a learned man?"

Though I knew he was teasing me, I was still embarrassed at my comment and felt heat creeping up my neck and spreading across my cheeks.

"Oh, no I apologize. I wasn't trying to insinuate—"

With a short chuckle he interrupted me and said, "Please, don't. I'm just giving you a hard time. I couldn't help overhearing your conversation and I agree with you. Writers should have the freedom to write about whatever they want and the public should be able to read it and share in it if they so choose."

He had managed to surprise me again with his apparent genuine deference toward literature. "I take it you're a fan of literature."

"That and all things related to education, really," he said as he grabbed a glass of champagne from a passing server.

I didn't recognize this man at all, and I usually at least knew of everyone at these types of events. His last comment, though, led me to believe that he was probably some sort of bureaucrat or involved in public policy in some form.

I couldn't deny that I was intrigued.

"Really?" I asked, studying him, "such as?" I was interested to see if he was going to try and feed me some rehearsed bullshit that he relayed to every person of influence he came across at political affairs. I didn't even know him but a lot of people would recognize me and try to get in good with my family. It was something I constantly had to deal with: dodging the ass-kissers.

He seemed to recognize the challenge in my voice as he straightened his shoulders, with an amused smirk on his face, and turned his body to better face mine, almost looking like he was squaring off with me. "Well, I'm a proponent of any type of educational reform that encourages more reading in schools. Not just in schools, either. I've been involved in several reading programs for adults, as well, particularly with the homeless. Most people don't realize the number of individuals in this city alone who either never learned how to read or just don't have the means to buy books, and I personally think that everyone should have that opportunity."

I stood there in front of him, unblinking, shocked. I certainly hadn't expected such an impassioned speech from him, and I honestly didn't know how to respond. I agreed with everything he said, but I just hadn't expected *that* to come out of his mouth. He looked satisfied that he'd surprised me, too.

"Did I pass your test?" he asked, that amused smirk still on his face.

"I—um," I stuttered. Wow, I was really having issues tonight. I shook my head, hoping that would make me think straight because I was probably looking like an idiot in front of the most gorgeous man I'd ever seen up close. "Test?" One word. *You sound very educated, Gwen. No more champagne for you.*

"Well, it seemed like you may have been making sure that I wasn't like everyone else here." His eyes flicked around the room briefly, indicating the other people in attendance.

I probably shouldn't have engaged him but I couldn't help it. "And what is everyone else here like?" I leaned slightly forward, anxious to hear his answer.

He leaned forward a little in my direction, his eyes darting around as if checking to make sure no one was listening, and said in a low voice, "Fake." He leaned back and met my eyes. I saw a playful gleam shining through his.

He was teasing me. Surprisingly, I found that I liked it, too.

I decided that I'd play along.

I put my hand over my chest mockingly. Feigning shock, I gasped, "Oh, you wouldn't dare say such things about the leaders of our community. How scandalous of you." He chuckled softly and I flashed him a warm smile. "Besides, I think they would probably prefer the term *charlatan*. Sounds so much more dignified, don't you think?"

His smile widened further and he nodded his head in approval. "Definitely. My mistake." His eyes turned more thoughtful as they briefly skirted down my body, sending tiny thrills through me everywhere he looked. "You act like you're pretty familiar with this scene."

I let out a sarcastic huff before I could stop myself. "It feels like too familiar some days." *Crap, why had I said that?* For all I knew, this man was a reporter and would print everything I said.

No, he's not a reporter. His stature spoke of someone who commanded the presence of everyone in any room he was in. A man with a plan, not a tape recorder.

He nodded his head knowingly and responded, "I know what you mean."

My head jerked back a bit at that, unprepared for his honesty. "You do?"

He nodded again, a timid smile curling his lips, making him look more boyish than manly. I found it adorable. His head swiveled about, taking in the room.

Prosperity and affluence. Wealth and privilege. That's what I saw as I followed his line of sight around the conglomeration of people that I was supposed to support. A group of people I was supposed to trust. A group that I had unwillingly become a member of. The thought made my stomach turn.

I wonder what he saw.

His expression turned serious. "Sometimes this can all feel a little suffocating. The dinners, the media circus, the interviews." His voice was a little harder than before, his posture more rigid. "It would be nice to be invisible every now and then."

My thoughts exactly. I was oddly comforted by his proclamation. Maybe I wasn't the only one who got sick of this life. I smiled at the thought. "And what exactly would you do if you were invisible?"

His head snapped back to mine, seeming momentarily surprised by the question. But then his eyes turned contemplative as he considered his answer. With a soft chuckle and an easy smile, he replied, "Cut to the front of every line at amusement parks, eat buffalo wings without a napkin, and skinny dip in the Reflecting Pool at the National Mall."

I couldn't help it. I burst into laughter. He beamed a bright, toothy smile at my reaction. Once again, I hadn't anticipated *that* answer. I had to admit his humor was refreshing in this setting. And just like that, I forgot who I was. Forgot how I was supposed to behave. In that moment, we were just a man and a woman having a conversation about nothing important and enjoying each other's company.

And it felt great.

"Well, let me know if you ever figure out the secret to invisibility and I'll be right there with you. Maybe not the skinny dipping part but I do love wings and rollercoasters," I said, still trying to get my laughter under control.

"And what about you? What would you do if you were invisible?" he asked, his eyes searching mine with a level of intensity that wasn't there before.

I suddenly became aware of how close we were standing and how good he smelled. I could feel his body heat even through all the material of our clothes, and it made my insides spark to life. It was a reaction I wasn't very familiar with because I never allowed myself to feel that way towards any man. There was no sense in getting worked up and wishing for things that could never be.

But with this man…I couldn't seem to stop myself from drowning in his magnitude. Because he had it. In spades, he had it.

Drawing my attention back to our conversation, I considered his question. *What would I do if I were invisible?* I really didn't have to think hard for an answer. It was a relatively uncomplicated, but honest one. I shrugged my shoulders and looked away from his gaze, needing some distance in order to voice the private thoughts I was about to reveal. "I would probably just walk around the city by myself. Have an entire day to enjoy all my favorite sights and not be hounded by reporters or anyone else. Where no one could interrupt my thoughts. Just bask in the peace and quiet, I guess."

Oh my God, he probably thought that was such a stupid answer. He wanted to skinny dip and I just wanted to walk around alone. Way to sound interesting, Gwen.

I mentally scoffed at myself, embarrassed at my lack of imagination, but he surprised me again. "That sounds perfect," he said. His voice was a beautiful husk and his gaze was penetrating me so deeply, it made heat rush to my face, making me blush under his scrutiny. But not in a bad way, though. Not at all.

The fact that he didn't laugh or tease me about my answer made my heart melt. Apparently to him, boring sounded perfect. I was okay with that.

Who knew that I would actually enjoy myself tonight? And with another man, no less? A man that I hoped William wouldn't see me talking to because he certainly would not approve. If this man had been older or uglier or had a woman with him, he may not have cared as much, but this stranger was breathtaking.

But I didn't want to think about William's reaction because I liked talking to this guy. Being around him was oddly comfortable. I couldn't explain that since I was never very comfortable around people I didn't know very well, especially men.

Then, he held out his hand to me and said, "I'm Clay Masterson." And my good mood vanished instantly.

Oh, no. I knew that name. My fiancé's nemesis. The one person standing in his way to becoming mayor. My insides tightened and I felt sick.

I took his outstretched hand, his large fingers closing tightly around mine. "Gwen McKindry."

His hand stilled at my name, his smile fading, and held on for a second or two too long. His eyes sparked with what looked like recognition, which was then confirmed when he said, "Ah, yes. You're William Callahan's..." he paused briefly and looked down at my ring finger for the first time, "...fiancé?"

"Yes. And you're his...opponent, I believe?" I tried to hide my disappointment at that revelation but with little success. This meant that I definitely shouldn't be talking to him. William would blow a fuse.

"It appears so," he said right before his face hardened and his eyes looked in the direction behind me.

That's when I felt a large hand at my hip, which instantly tightened and gripped me hard, causing me to wince slightly in pain. I had long ago learned to school my expressions in public when it came to William and his possessive manner, but this took me so off guard that I couldn't prevent my reaction.

Clay narrowed his eyes at the action, looking back and forth between William and me.

"I don't believe we've officially been introduced," William said cordially, but I could see the bulging veins in his neck and the throbbing of his pulse. He was pissed. *Great.* "William Callahan." He offered his hand to Clay.

Clay hesitated only a second and then took it, his lips barely curling up at the ends in an almost-grin. "Clay Masterson."

"Yes, of course. We meet at last, Mr. Masterson," William responded in a pompous tone with a cocky grin on his face.

Clay didn't seem perturbed by William's attitude. "It's certainly taken long enough, Mr. Callahan. Your fiancé and I were just discussing educational reform, actually."

Oh, crap. William's hand tightened on my hip—I'd probably have a bruise there tomorrow—and I could feel his entire body tense next to mine. Not only did he not like me talking to other men, but he especially didn't like me getting involved with his political agenda.

This was going downhill fast.

William's expression was stony when he replied, "Is that so?" He looked down at me then and all I saw was red hot fury emanating from his dark eyes. The smile that spread over his face was cold and menacing and sent a chill down my spine. It was a smile that promised punishment, which he already seemed to be contemplating, and delighting in. "Well, Gwen likes to stay involved. Don't you, dear?"

The look he gave me warned me not say anything I would regret. I forced a tight smile and said, "Anything I can do to help." I looked down at my feet. I couldn't look into William's threatening eyes any longer, and there was no way I was locking eyes with Clay, though I could feel his on me. All we had done was talk but I was afraid that William would see how much I had liked it if I looked up at my new acquaintance.

Clay looked like he was about to say something but before he could, William spoke up and said, "As a matter of fact, darling, I need your charm to work its magic on a few colleagues of mine over there." He tipped his head in the direction of a table across the room where several older gentlemen sat with glasses of brandy in their hands, their wives sitting opposite them and talking with their heads close together.

Of course, he was lying. He just wanted me close to him and away from Clay. This routine wasn't new.

"It was a pleasure, Mr. Masterson," William said in a clipped tone and nodded at Clay as he grabbed my elbow and started pulling me away.

"Likewise," Clay replied and then stepped forward and added, "it was a pleasure to meet you as well, Ms. McKindry." His eyes were intense as they gazed into mine and I was momentarily speechless. He had fire in his eyes and I wasn't sure if it was directed at me or William. Because everyone knew who I was, and because they all knew who I was engaged to, no man ever looked at me that way. They were too intimidated by William and for good reason.

But suddenly I couldn't look away from the man standing in front of me.

"You too, Mr. Masterson," I murmured, still in a minor state of shock. I finally looked away when William pulled on my arm again but Clay had still been staring at me. It made me smile on the inside.

As we walked across the room, William bent down until his mouth was

right at my ear and whispered harshly, "We'll talk about this later."

And just like that, every warm feeling that Clay had stirred up inside me was instantly obliterated.

Clay

I had seen her from across the room and hadn't been able to take my eyes off her. Even though her back had been facing me, I still thought that I should've recognized her if I'd seen her before because it was a very beautiful back. But I had no idea who she was.

Long, blonde hair falling down her slender back in loose curls, the deep scoop in her dress exposing skin that looked so silky and creamy I had wanted to lick every inch, and the curves around her ass were just perfect for my hands to grab on to. Yes, I had been sure I would have recognized her if I'd met her before. You couldn't forget a figure like that.

Suddenly, I had felt compelled to introduce myself. Surely, the front would be as gorgeous as the back, there's no way it couldn't be. I had excused myself from my conversation with two older gentlemen and headed in her direction.

And I honestly hadn't been expecting what I found.

She was *gorgeous. Exquisite.*

She had certainly put a whole new spin on *breathtaking* because I had to actually take a second to catch mine after I'd seen her face. What I'd been picturing in my head as I walked towards her in no way compared to the real thing. She was *that* stunning. High cheekbones, clear, dark blue eyes, flawless skin, and full red lips.

What drew me in even further was her scent. As soon as I'd gotten closer to her I could smell it. It was a tantalizing mixture of sweet and citrus—like vanilla and tangerine—and it had possibly been the most intoxicating fragrance I'd ever smelled on a woman. It made me want to lean in closer and see if she smelled like that all over. And when I say all over, I mean *all over*.

And she was smart. The conversation I had interrupted when I'd reached her was evidence that she was well-read, intelligent, and certainly not afraid to show it. It was refreshing and I found myself immediately intrigued. I had to admit that none of the last few women I'd dated had intrigued me. Not that I'd dated much recently, but I couldn't remember any of them capturing my interest the way she had.

Not only was she smart, but she'd also been sharp, perceptive and even funny. Not many people that ran in these elite circles had much of a sense of humor, and if they did, I was rarely amused. But she did and it had surprised me. What had me even more perplexed was how easy it had been to be around her. As soon as we started talking I'd felt like we'd already known each other for years, which was nice but different. It had only heightened my curiosity.

It'd been obvious that she wasn't new to this type of crowd but, in fact, had been around it for some time. And for all of her sarcastic humor and disinterest in the social scene around her, I could sense a certain sadness about her beneath the mask she tried to cover it with. It probably worked with everyone else, too, because so many of these people were oblivious to the entire spectrum of human emotion. But I saw through it. And as messed up as it sounded, it only endeared me to her that much more.

Even after a few minutes of talking, I still hadn't recognized her, but I hadn't cared at the time because I'd been content to just talk to her for a while. I'd eventually get her name and hopefully, a number.

Then I did get her name, and any hopes of getting her number, or continuing our conversation tonight at my place like I'd been envisioning, had been immediately crushed. And it surprised me how disappointed I had been at that realization.

Of course, the first woman in a long time that I'd been truly interested in was engaged, and to my competition, no less. I knew of William Callahan, and I'd heard that he was engaged to a McKindry, but I didn't know who Gwen actually was. I'd always heard the McKindry name—that was a given if you lived in D.C.—but I'd never seen a picture of her. And I had to admit that I couldn't believe that the down-to-earth, captivating woman I'd been talking to, and flirting with, was part of the McKindry clan. Most of what I'd been told about that particular family was never favorable. My father had once been acquainted with Howard McKindry, Gwen's father, and he always said that he'd never liked the man, though I wasn't sure why.

And it was quite clear that William Callahan didn't like his fiancé talking to me at all. I'd immediately sensed the tension in the relationship, it didn't exactly look like a happy one. I could tell that he wanted to get her away from me as quickly as possible and, maybe it was wishful thinking on my part, but she almost looked reluctant to go with him. I'd immediately gotten a bad feeling about the guy and had found it very difficult to be polite to him. And he hadn't exactly looked like he wanted to go have a beer with me either. That was okay, though, because I didn't need to like the guy. I just needed to beat him in the election.

What had been even more obvious than his dislike for me was that William was very possessive of his fiancé. I hadn't missed the grip he'd had on her the whole time we were talking, and I had caught Gwen's reaction even if she had quickly masked it—the bastard had been hurting her and she hadn't looked the least bit surprised by it.

Without realizing it, my hands had turned into fists at my sides, and it took me everything I had to keep from grabbing the other man by his throat and throwing him into the buffet table. And then beat the ever-loving shit out of him. I didn't really understand this reaction, though. I had just met the woman but I was already feeling a sense of protectiveness towards her. I just had this feeling that she needed to someone to look out for her and strangely enough, *I* wanted to be the man doing it.

But she's engaged.

I sighed at the thought. I never went after another man's woman. That was an unbreakable rule for me. But this one felt different somehow. I couldn't explain it but I had a nagging urge to get close to her, like I was *supposed* to get close to her or something, which didn't make any sense at all. In fact, it was ridiculous. I just had to forget about meeting her and that whole encounter because she was with someone, and the nature of their relationship wasn't any of my business. I didn't need to get involved whatsoever.

An hour and a few conversations later—despite my attempts not to do so—my mind kept drifting back to a certain blue-eyed blonde. My eyes searched the ballroom for the only person I found myself actually wanting to talk to, but I didn't see her. I couldn't explain why, but I hadn't wanted to end our earlier conversation. I had an odd feeling that I could have talked to her all night and would have enjoyed every minute of it.

If that prick hadn't interrupted us, I would have been able to find out more about her. Yes, I had been somewhat crestfallen to discover she was engaged, though I should have expected it. These types of events weren't bars, not many single attractive women attended them unescorted. Most were either married, engaged, or seriously dating someone there.

As I walked toward the entrance of the building, I stopped in my tracks when I saw her. She was standing on the sidewalk outside the entrance door with her head downcast, her bastard fiancé looking down at her with a look of barely contained rage, obviously scolding her but trying not to make a scene. My jaw clenched so tight at the sight, I would have felt pain if I had been paying attention to anything other than her.

Her mouth opened and moved slightly as if she was whispering something, at which point William's hands flew up and roughly grabbed her upper arms, yanking her to him. He didn't seem to care that he could be seen by anyone who just happened to look towards the door, or anyone out on the street.

I saw red. A fury-fueled haze clouded my vision and my blood started to boil throughout my entire body. If that asshole wanted to get aggressive, I'd sure as hell get aggressive with him. I hated men who thought they could bully women, physically or mentally. It was one of the few things I just couldn't stand for and felt like I had to do something whenever I saw it, no matter who it was. The fact that I had felt some sort of strange connection with this woman just augmented the situation.

Before I could stop myself, I was walking briskly towards the door with rage propelling me forward. I knew it wasn't my place to interfere but I would make him remove his hands if he didn't calm down. Fiancé or not.

Before I could reach the doors, though, a black town car abruptly stopped in front of them, and William whipped open the door with one hand while his other held tightly onto Gwen. Without another word, he practically threw her into the backseat, which only further served to piss me off. William then climbed inside after her and the car sped off.

I had stopped at the front doors with my hand white knuckling the handle as I watched the car speed down the street, then turn around a corner and out of sight. I let go of the handle and took a few deep breaths, needing to get myself under control. I had almost just let my emotions get the better of me, and had almost allowed myself to do something that was so monumentally stupid, I had to wonder if I'd had more to drink tonight than I thought. Attacking the man I was running against was the worst possible thing I could have done.

Flirting with his fiancé hadn't exactly been smart either.

Okay, no it hadn't been, but I hadn't known she was his fiancé.

Maybe it was time that I learned a little bit more about William Callahan.

CHAPTER FOUR

A TOWER AND A FIRE-BREATHING POLITICIAN

Gwen

I sat at the writing desk in my lounge hammering away at my laptop with the newest chapter in my book. William never came in here so I decorated the room to my liking and thought of it as *my* lounge. I came in here when I wanted to write, read a book, or just decompress from the emotional turmoil that I felt enveloped in on a daily basis.

The loveseat that sat in the room was a sage green and was so comfortable that I'd take naps in it when I needed a break from the world. A brown antique trunk served as my coffee table and sat in front of the loveseat. I'd found it at an estate sale three years ago and adored it on sight. It looked like it had so much history and I would never be able to part with it.

The six foot tall bookcase that held all my favorite books stood against the opposite wall of my writing desk. Its white paint was chipped and falling off, so the color of the wood was a mixture between off-white and sand. It had a lot of character and was another piece that I would forever cherish. It was also an antique, one I found at a small, hole-in-the-wall antique store in Georgetown just last year before William and I got engaged.

But my writing desk was the piece of furniture in the room that meant the most to me. It was buttercup yellow with plenty of dents and chips that made me feel cozy every time I used it because it felt lived in, it felt like home. It was more than special to me because my grandmother left it to me before she died.

My grandmother was the only family member I had who had seemed to love me unconditionally. No matter what I wore, what I said or how I acted, I knew I was loved by that woman, and I had cherished every moment I was able to spend with her growing up and as an adult.

She was also the only person who had ever supported my writing. Grandma had always encouraged my ideas and dreams and always wanted to read what I wrote. Apparently she had liked to write too, mostly poems and short stories, which was the reason why she left me her desk. It was probably my most prized possession.

I lost my grandmother to old age a little over three years ago, right before William and I started dating, and the desk was all I had left of the woman other than a few pictures.

On the walls were paintings of some of my favorite places around the world, though I hadn't been to any of them. They were just random landscapes that I had collected over the years because they made me happy and relaxed whenever I looked at them. Sure, I wanted to go to all of them and I often imagined what it would be like if I could. To run along the white sand beaches in Bermuda, splashing in the crystal clear waters. To roll around in the long, green grass that stretched for miles across the Irish countryside. To ski down the rugged, snowcapped Alps. To fly among the swirling clouds on a warm summer day, floating so high above everyone and everything else in the world.

It all sounded like heaven to me. I would often sit in my favorite plush lounge chair by the two French windows—the floor to ceiling panes of glass were the most spectacular feature of the room—wrapped up in my warmest blanket, and create another life for myself in each of these places. Whether I was staring out the window into space, had my nose stuck in a novel, or was brainstorming new book ideas, I felt at peace in my chair by the window. I sat at my desk specifically to write but when I was in my chair, I could imagine anything, dream of anything, hope for anything.

This room was my sanctuary and I thanked God every day that William continued to allow me to have it all to myself and to do whatever I wanted with it. Whenever we had guests over, they were never allowed in here if I could help it. It was only mine.

I was working on my book in that moment because I *needed* to write. Writing soothed me and took my mind to worlds not my own. I had actually written several full-length novels—all in the horror, thriller, or suspense genres—but hadn't even attempted to publish any of them. William would never approve of or allow it. Same with my parents.

It might seem odd that I wrote stories with a horror or suspense element, and most people would probably never suspect that I was interested in those particular genres. But most people didn't know me. I had always been fascinated in the unknown and with the many figures and situations that scare people or make them uncomfortable. I couldn't explain where the allure stemmed from, but for some reason, those stories had always clicked with me and if I were allowed, I could write for days on end about it, developing my plots and characters.

Nobody else other than my grandmother had ever read any of my work. I expressed my interest in writing to my parents when I was young, and they immediately discouraged the idea. Actually, they forbade me to spend my time pursuing such a "menial vocation." Honestly, I thought my writing was pretty good, but I didn't think I could bear it if I sent my books off to a publisher and they told me that I was terrible. The only people even in my life that might be willing to read my work were my friends Beatrice and Felicity, but something still held me back from letting them into my private world of fiction. It almost felt like if I shared it with anyone, if I let others in, then it would no longer be my refuge, my sanctuary.

I also wasn't sure how William would react if I told him that I wanted to seriously pursue writing, but I had a fairly good idea that it wouldn't be pleasant. He would probably say something similar to what my parents had said, that it wasn't the sort of thing that a McKindry/Callahan did.

Regardless, I was still able to write and get my ideas on paper. Writing itself served as a sort of therapy for my mind, so it didn't really matter whether my stories were read by others or not. All of my main characters were damaged in some way or another, and if I wanted to be introspective, I could admit that perhaps it was my own past and present manifesting themselves in my stories. At least, that's probably what a therapist would tell me.

Expressing my thoughts and emotions through my characters provided an outlet for me that didn't exist anywhere else in my life. I didn't have anyone to whom I could open up or rely on to protect my secrets, so I spoke through my books. Which was probably why I hadn't let anyone ever read them. I had never trusted anyone enough to let them see that far into my psyche. I trusted Beatrice and Felicity, of course, but even though I loved both of them like sisters, they still didn't know everything about me. My darkest thoughts, my greatest fears, my deepest emotions. I just never felt like I could open up completely to them.

And tonight, I needed therapy in the worst way. William had unsurprisingly berated me for my conversation with Clay at the dinner, which had left me shaky, empty, and exhausted by the time he was done. Then, he stormed out the front door to God knows where. Probably going to one of the exclusive strip clubs that he frequented to release his "tension." The thought made my whole body shudder. *Ick.*

I didn't exactly have much of a say in our sexual relationship as it was, and I couldn't remember the last time he had actually put in the effort to pleasure me. *Had he ever pleasured me?* I really didn't know.

How sad that was.

I'd been surprised at William's reaction on the sidewalk earlier in the evening. He never raised his voice to me in public—there was always someone with a camera phone nearby who was all too ready to sell a video or picture to the media—and for a minute, I thought he was actually going to do something more than just yell at me. But he contained himself and instead threw me into the car so hard that I slid across the leather seat and almost hit my head on the opposite door.

He hadn't said anything else in the car on the way home, and I'd kept my eyes glued to my hands in my lap, trying to physically and mentally prepare myself for whatever awaited me at home. My eyes had darted up a few times to see how close to the house we were, and I'd seen Roberto glancing back at us in the rearview mirror with a concerned expression on his face.

For the most part, he knew that William took his temper out on me, though probably not to the full extent, and he worried about me a lot and told me as much. I felt bad that he wanted to help me but I also knew he needed this job to help support his family, so I always told him that I was perfectly fine.

When we had arrived home, William stomped through the front door and went straight to his study where his whiskey waited for him. He knocked a few shots back before he turned to me with black, menacing eyes and I knew I was in for it.

All of a sudden, he slammed his glass down so hard on his desk he almost shattered it and then stalked across the room, straight toward me. He stopped in front of me and, without preamble, slapped me so hard across my cheek my vision went black for a few seconds. "What the fuck were you doing talking to my biggest opponent?" he roared.

I'd been momentarily shocked by his action but recovered quickly. He'd only hit me a couple of times before, always with an open hand instead of a closed fist—not that that made it in any way excusable—and it was typically when he was at his most angry. Alcohol was usually involved, copious amounts of it.

My cheek was on fire and I lightly rubbed it with one hand, trying to ease the pain. I had learned it was best to take his anger and never talk back because it always made it ten times worse. In a meek voice I replied, "It was just a polite introduction. We hadn't been talking but a few minutes before you came over and it was only about the campaign. I promise."

His eyes flared at my words. "I saw the way he was looking at you. He wanted you and you know how that makes me feel, Gwen." He sounded absolutely murderous. I shrunk away from him even more and wrapped my arms around my waist, as if that would protect me from him.

"Yes, but I promise that he didn't flirt and he knew I was engaged to you. You know I wouldn't do anything like that." Placating him in these situations was always best, to tamp down his anger a bit.

"I know because you know what would happen, don't you? I would hurt him and then I would hurt you."

I knew that he meant every word he said, too. He was possessive and jealous enough that he would probably hurt me without a second thought, and then go after whichever man he thought I was having an affair with.

These were the times that I thought he might be more unstable that I initially thought. He would never admit to it, but there were rumors in some circles that William's father had been treated for bipolar disorder at some point in his life, and I wasn't convinced that William didn't suffer from the same condition. It would certainly explain his mood swings and violent outbursts.

He hadn't gotten more physically violent with me than a couple slaps on the face—and the rough sex he would subject me to when he was in these moods—but I was becoming more and more worried that his behavior was escalating and things would get worse before they got better. *Isn't that what usually happens in these situations?*

"I know but you have nothing to worry about."

"I better not, Gwen. You're mine, do you understand me? You're mine to do whatever the hell I want with." His lips curled into a hideous snarl. His face was directly in front of mine, his body painfully pushing mine against the wall.

He grabbed both sides of my face, his fingers sliding through and then roughly pulling on my hair. He brought his face to within an inch of my own and whispered, "To touch," his tongue came out and licked along my jawline, "to use," his mouth moved to my earlobe where his teeth clamped down, making me cry out in pain, "to *fuck*, however I want."

As he said the last, he yanked my head back by my hair and slammed his lips down onto mine with such force it pushed me further against the wall, knocking the breath out of me.

"You know what I would do if anyone touched this, Gwen." His hand left my hair to slide along my inner thigh, going higher and higher. I swallowed down the bile that was threatening to come up. "You know what I would do if anyone touched what was mine."

He ended the statement with his hand grabbing onto my sex through my dress and rubbing it so hard, I couldn't stop a tear from escaping and falling down my cheek.

"This is mine, Gwen, and you will give it to me whenever I want it." He was starting to rub me raw and he hadn't even taken me yet. *This is going to be a rough one.* "I don't want you talking to other men or touching other men, especially Clay Masterson. And if I see you doing either I will make you regret it."

His words and the tone of his voice sent shivers down my spine, causing my whole body start to shake in fear. Then, he took my lips again in a brutal, bruising kiss. Before I could even react, he bit down on my bottom lip so hard I whimpered and jerked my head away. My tongue licked over where he had bitten down and already I tasted blood.

"Were you hoping to get some male attention tonight by wearing this dress, my dear?" His voice was callous and mocking, his fingers sliding into the slit of my dress. "Did you want them to imagine finger fucking you through this slit? Lifting the material up until they felt your pussy and then sliding their fingers into you?"

All of a sudden he ripped my slit even further, exposing my naked body up to the lace thong I wore, the ripping of the material echoing in the quiet room. He pushed my underwear aside and shoved two large fingers inside me. More tears escaped as I released silent sobs.

"Because I can easily do that for you, Gwen," he whispered in my ear as he roughly thrust his fingers in and out of me.

Then, he abruptly pulled out his fingers and spun me around by my shoulders so my front was pressed against the wall. I could feel his arousal pushing against my backside, and I tried to send my mind to one of the places in my lounge paintings. Anything to escape the feel of his hands on my body.

"Or did you leave your back bare like this so they could imagine taking you from behind, bending you over one of those tables and slamming into so hard you screamed? Huh? Were those your whorish fantasies? Are you a little whore, Gwen?" He had started off whispering but he was practically shouting now.

He started thrusting his hips, forcing his erection into my crack. He had taken me there before, even though I begged him not to because I knew he would be rough. He had been and I had hated every second of it. I had bled and was sore for days after.

"Please, William," I pleaded, "please, stop."

"Shut up!" he yelled in my ear and dug his fingers into my hips even harder. "I own you! I'll do what I want and you'll take it because I OWN YOU!" He was in full crazy mode now.

With that, he grabbed my upper arms, dragging me away from the wall and over to his desk. With one hand on the back of my head and one hand on my lower back, he bent me over the desk so my front was smashed against the surface.

I felt a sharp pain pierce my chest, right between my breasts, and realized that he had pushed me on top of the ceramic paper weight my parents had given William as a gift when he won the primary election back in April. It was digging into my skin so hard I couldn't help the shriek of pain that left my mouth when he leaned over me, his mouth right at my ear, putting all of his weight on top of me.

"Well, if that's what you want, you little slut, I'll give it to you." He reeked of sweat and whiskey and I wanted to throw up. It wouldn't be the first time I had after he'd taken me. "But you're going to remember who you belong to. You're going to remember who's fucking you like this and who will be the *only* one ever fucking you like this."

He grabbed both of my wrists and wrenched them behind my back, holding them with one hand while his other lifted up my dress. I could hear the sickening clanking sound of his belt buckle and subsequent zipper being pulled down.

Go to one of your happy places.

I could feel him guide himself to my entrance—thankfully not the one I dreaded him taking again—and started to push in with all of his force. I was as dry as the Mojave Desert. I always was when he took me and it hurt. A lot.

I bit my lip to keep from screaming because it would only spur him on, and I let my mind wander to one of my beloved paintings. I was standing on a gorgeous cliffside, looking out across a vast terrain of forests interspersed with sparkling rivers that reminded me of tears streaming down a face. There were rolling green hills stretching across the horizon and the sun was beating down on me, as if it were bringing everything to life, including me.

I barely heard William's grunts and groans as he continued to pound into me from behind, could barely feel the pain of the paper weight as it dug into my skin. I kept my eyes tightly shut and I could practically feel the sun beating down on me from on top of that cliff. In my head, I lifted my arms skyward and let the sun rejuvenate me, taking away the pain and the loneliness.

William released one last shout as he finished inside me but didn't immediately release me. Instead, he bent down again and said in an eerily calm voice, "I fucking own you, Gwen. You can't escape me. *Ever*. I'm never letting you go."

He breathed in sharply and said slowly, "I. Own. You."

I winced as he pulled out of me, in no way gentle. I stayed bent over the desk with my eyes still squeezed shut as I listened to him pulling his pants back up and righting the rest of his clothing. He didn't say another word as he left the room and a few seconds later was out the front door, slamming it closed behind him.

It took me a minute to find the strength to push myself up from the desk. Releasing myself from the pressure of the paper weight hurt more than I'd thought it would. I looked down and saw a round indentation in my skin the size of a quarter, the skin already turning purple. That was going to leave one heck of a bruise.

I took a long, hot bath after that, scrubbing my skin raw in an attempt to remove any remnant of his smell or touch, though I knew this never worked. I would always have those images and his words in my mind later, but it made me feel a little better, if only for a short time. The bath also helped ease some of the ache in my muscles and a few other sensitive places that I tried to ignore.

I knew what most people would think of me if they knew what went on behind our closed doors. They would probably say that I was a foolish, blind, *weak* woman. I had never considered myself to be a weak person and thought that I had actually turned out pretty well considering I had to endure having parents like mine.

But William made me feel just that: weak.

I didn't want to be like that but I couldn't help it. Every time that man got angry with me and stood in front of me, his cold, black eyes boring holes through me, I froze. Fear made my muscles lock up and my mouth clamp shut. My mind would be screaming at me to fight back, to run away, to do *something*, but panic and fear always won out. As much as I hated to admit it, William terrified me. He was unpredictable, a loose cannon, and all I ever wanted was to stay out of the line of fire.

Never in a million years did I ever expect to end up in an abusive relationship with a man whom I could never love and who would never love me. It had always bewildered me that so many women who suffered spousal, or any kind of domestic, abuse would willingly stay in those relationships. How their minds had become so warped that they would continuously endure that type of treatment, I didn't know. Well, I hadn't known, until William.

He wasn't like this every night. These nights were usually the result of excessive drinking on his part, the stress of his job getting to him, or something I had done that he didn't approve of. Or like tonight, it had been a combination of all three.

Even though he had only ever slapped me and taken me roughly, that wasn't to say that he didn't leave marks on me because he definitely did at times. He never left bruises on my face because his hand only ever left a red mark which faded by the next day. But the bruises that he left on other parts of my body from taking me too aggressively were occasionally a problem. I couldn't wear sleeveless tops after he grabbed my arms like he did tonight. I couldn't wear shorts for several days after he'd gotten particularly rough one night because he left several bruises on my inner thighs that would have looked very questionable.

Though I no longer tried to resist him when he got in these moods, it didn't mean that I hadn't fought him in the beginning. Well, I'd tried to, anyway. After he slapped me the first time, he'd been immediately remorseful and begged me to forgive him. He'd literally gotten down on his knees and hugged my waist. I had been so shocked that he'd actually raised his hand to me that all I could do was stroke his hair and tell him that I forgave him. He seemed so disgusted with himself that I'd actually believed that he wouldn't do it again.

I'd been wrong.

Believe it or not, though, I had real feelings for William once. Even though my parents pushed the relationship on me, I had allowed myself to care for William after we started dating. In the early stages of our relationship, he'd been a completely different man. He'd been affectionate and doted on me, like I was precious to him. He'd taken me out on frequent dates and I actually enjoyed his company. I had begun to convince myself that marrying him wouldn't be so bad, though I never actually loved him.

Then he changed. I couldn't pinpoint the exact time it had started or what the cause of it was, but it was like he just snapped one day. He started becoming more distant, rarely took me out, and was much quicker to get angry with me.

When he hit me the first time, I'd known it wasn't right, but I excused it because I cared for him and I assumed that he had just been stressed and momentarily lashed out. When he did it the second time, though, I got angry. Once again, he had been apologetic and begged for my forgiveness. Instead of comforting him, though, that time I'd yelled at him and said I was going to leave him.

That's when the begging stopped. The broken look in his eyes had been instantly replaced by hardened fury and he went toe-to-toe with me, straightening up to his tallest form. It had definitely been intimidating. That was when he'd scared me so much that I was too afraid to even think about leaving him again. He'd basically told me that he would never let me leave him, no matter what. I was his and things weren't going to change.

Not to mention the fact that he'd said if I ever tried to leave him, he would taint mine and my family's name so horridly in the press that we would never be accepted in D.C. society again. The Callahans were an institution in this city and they had connections everywhere. Anything they wanted, they got and no questions were asked. I didn't care so much about my reputation, but my parents would care immensely for the McKindry name, and there would be harsh consequences for me if I messed things up for them.

Even though I had been freaked out, I'd still went to my parents and begged them to get me out of the engagement. I shouldn't have been surprised, but when they insisted that I was exaggerating things and that William loved me and would never harm me, I'd been speechless. They had said that the marriage was too good of an opportunity for both families and that it would simply be ridiculous and poor judgment to cancel the wedding.

So, I'd found a way to remove myself from the situation in a way and compartmentalize everything. I knew I'd go crazy if I didn't. I'd clung onto hope that maybe someday an opportunity would come and I'd be able to escape William and have a different, better life. Common sense kept nagging at me, trying to convince me that would never happen as long as I was bound to him, but the hope of a happier future had kept my body from breaking and kept my mind sane.

Despite all of it, I knew that deep down I was still strong and I still had a certain resolve to live that I would never allow William to take away from me. He could use me as hard and as often as he liked, but I vowed that I would never lose myself, my personality, my mind, my heart, or my soul, to William Callahan. He might use me in every reprehensible way possible but I would never truly be his.

My willpower kept me strong. Kept me from succumbing to complete submission. It kept me alive.

After my bath, I'd changed into my silk lounge pants and cotton tank, locked myself in my lounge to write and hadn't come out since. I knew

William wouldn't be back until the early morning and I'd make sure that I was tucked into bed long before that.

Even though he'd been the cause of William's explosive rage, I couldn't prevent my mind from conjuring up images of Clay or thinking about our earlier conversation. I didn't recognize the spike of adrenalin or the increase in my pulse every time I thought of him. The way he'd smiled at me, his sharp wit, and the inexplicable way my body reacted to his. No man had ever made me feel like that.

It had been easy to talk to him, comfortable even. He'd made me feel at ease in an environment that always felt claustrophobic, like my back was up against the wall. For a politician, he'd seemed uncharacteristically carefree and laid-back, even while he was right in the middle of the lion's den. Whatever it meant, talking to him just felt so *right.*

I couldn't deny that I loved that feeling.

Heat had spread throughout my entire body, from my head straight down to my toes, during our conversation and I was experiencing the same sensation just by thinking about him. Even though I didn't have a lot of experience with this sort of thing, I knew what I was feeling was attraction and desire.

But I wouldn't allow it. *Couldn't* allow it. I could never act on it so I didn't even want to think about getting my hopes up. The most I could do was cast him in the starring role of my private fantasies and that was it.

I wouldn't lie to myself, though. I didn't know this man at all, but I already wanted more from him. I'd always wanted to fall hard for someone, to feel breathless in their presence. To experience what real love was supposed to look and feel like. I wanted to feel giddy, anxious, impatient. I wanted to feel all those emotions that new relationships brought. I wanted to feel adored, cared for, cherished. I wanted those feelings of puppy love to blossom into something lasting and meaningful.

I wanted to feel loved.

It seemed like such a simple concept, yet it had always been unattainable to me. I wasn't a fool. I wouldn't let my attraction to this man cloud my common sense. I knew that only led to mistakes, and mistakes in my world held close company with danger.

I closed my laptop once I realized my head was a million miles away from what I was working on. I allowed myself one last fantasy of Clay as I lay in bed that night, staring up at the ceiling, before I would completely erase him from my mind.

In my fantasy, he stood with me on that cliffside, holding my hand, and soaking up the sun with me. He just stood beside me with his eyes closed, offering warmth and comfort merely with his presence. It wasn't a grand romantic gesture or anything but I didn't really need that. It was comforting enough to feel, even for a minute, like I wasn't entirely alone in this world.

With these thoughts swirling around in my head, I was able to slip into the most peaceful sleep I'd had in months.

CHAPTER FIVE

OBLIGATIONS AND INVITATIONS

Gwen

The next day I had wedding planning and lunch scheduled with probably the only two people in the world of snotty socialites and power-hungry politicians that I could actually stand to be around. Well, aside from Clay Masterson, it would seem.

Beatrice and Felicity Paxton were the epitome of Southern belles, with their big voices, sweet-natured charms, and boisterous accents. Beatrice was a tall brunette with a lean, athletic build, and Felicity was small and petite, like a little pixie fairy with her blonde hair cut into a fashionable bob. Both women were insanely gorgeous.

They may have come from old, Southern money, but they were some of the most down-to-earth people I'd ever met. How they managed to grow up richer than God with a family name that had become a veritable household name in the political world and yet stay as humble and likeable as they were, was absolutely beyond me. I didn't have many friends because I couldn't stand the whole persona and attitude of the social elite, so I deeply cherished the friendship that I had with these two women.

Today, they were coming with me to help me pick out invitations at the designer my mother was forcing me to hire. Supposedly, "everyone who matters in D.C." went to them for wedding invitations. After that, we had to go by the caterer's business to try some dishes and were going to be provided with lunch, which sounded so much more enjoyable to me than designing ugly invitations that were just going to eventually get thrown away.

It was disappointing, really, how unexcited I was to be planning my own wedding. When I was young, I, like every other little girl, dreamed of what my wedding would one day look like. I dreamed of a beautiful flowing dress, roses everywhere, and having a handsome man waiting at the end of the isle for me. Of course, back then that beautiful man looked exactly like my Ken doll because he was the only boy I could imagine marrying at the time.

As I grew up, my idea of what my wedding would look like changed, like any girl's did, but one thing always remained constant in all of those images: I was happy. I looked happy in my dress, with all of my friends and family surrounding me, and my groom, whoever he was, looked just as happy as me. In those dreams, it was the best day of my life and was the beginning of something new and exciting.

It was *not* marrying somebody that I couldn't stand and having almost every detail of the event chosen for me. My mother, as always, was driving me nuts with the planning. My opinion didn't matter and it was always her decision in the end. She'd made it clear many times that it was her and my father's money paying for the wedding, so she should have some control in the process.

Some control? Try *complete* control.

Not that I cared anymore. I got over the idea of wanting to plan my own wedding pretty quickly because what was the point if I wasn't even in love with the groom? My mother could plan all the details she wanted because I had no desire whatsoever to do so. I was actually surprised that she was allowing me to handle the arrangements scheduled for today without her. Well, more to the point, she *ordered* that I take care of things today, offering up no other option but to listen to her. She had some other business to take care of, but I'm sure that if she doesn't approve of what I select, she'll just change it to what she wants later.

I stepped out of the car in front of the graphic designer's building and saw Beatrice and Felicity standing on the sidewalk, waiting. When they saw me, both of their mouths spread into huge smiles and they held out their arms to hug me.

"Don't you just look down right scrumptious today," Beatrice crooned in her sing-song voice as she held out my arms and looked me up and down.

"Yeah, who's the lucky devil?" Felicity smiled mischievously at her. Neither of them knew the extent of William's abhorrent behavior, but they knew enough about him to not like him. At all. They knew how I felt about the situation, too, and they were the only people I could ever talk to about it.

They were true friends. The only ones I had.

"Please," I scoffed, rolling my eyes at their comments. I looked no different than any other day. "It's hot out and I wanted to be comfortable if we're going to stuff our faces later."

Picking out my outfit today was actually a little challenging because I had to cover up the bruises on my thighs and hips—courtesy of William—so I couldn't wear short shorts or a short top, but I also couldn't wear anything with short sleeves because of the bruises he left on my upper arms. But it was also hot out and I refused to suffer a heat stroke because my fiancé was insane. I ended up going with a turquoise maxi dress and a kimono-style cardigan to go over it, so the bruises would be covered and the light material would still give me some breathing room. I just couldn't take it off.

"Oh, yes, praise Jesus. Please tell me that alcohol will be included in the beverages we'll be samplin'," Beatrice said hopefully.

"I don't know but I'm sure I'll need it by that point. Maybe if you bat your eyelashes enough and say sweet nothings in that accent of yours, you might be able to swipe us a couple bottles of wine," I teased.

Beatrice had always been the perpetual flirt of the group, and she'd scored us more than a few free drinks in the past. Felicity was more of the sweet and shy type, with her petite figure and mousy face. She was adorable. And I, of course, was engaged so anytime we three went out together—which usually resulted in a fight with William—the course of the evening typically followed with Beatrice hitting on one or several guys and Felicity and I entertaining ourselves at a corner table or on the dance floor. We always had fun, though, and I loved being around them.

"Well my girls are really workin' for me today, so I'll see what I can do," she said as she pulled her already low cut top down even further while pushing her boobs up at the same time.

Felicity and I gave each other a look as I rolled my eyes but couldn't stop the smile from spreading across my face. This was exactly what I needed today.

"Uh-huh and if you pull that shirt down any more, everybody will be seeing what you can do," Felicity quipped and I laughed as we walked through the doors and into the reception area.

The young girl sitting behind the reception desk greeted us with a smile as we approached and greeted us. "Good afternoon, ladies. How may I help you?"

"I have an appointment with Ms. Van der Holden. I'm Gwen McKindry."

Recognition sparked in the girl's eyes at my name and she instantly popped up from her chair. "Oh yes, of course, Miss McKindry. I'll let Ms. Van der Holden know you're here. Please make yourselves comfortable," she politely said, indicating the chairs behind us as she took off down the hallway to the right.

"Well, this place looks...stately," Beatrice mused as she took in our surroundings.

It really did and not in a good way. There were expensive furnishings covering every inch of the room. The Persian rugs we were standing on, the gold filigree-laden vases and mirrors, the crystal chandelier above our heads. It looked more like the Palace at Versailles, not a graphic design company.

We heard the click of heels on the floor heading in our direction before we had a chance to sit down. I looked up and saw a prim, middle-aged woman walking towards me. Her brown hair was pulled back in an elegant twist, her skin was pale, and she wore a pristine pale yellow pantsuit. She was attractive and her smile was pleasant enough, but I could already sense a certain aloofness about her.

"Hello, Miss McKindry. I'm Ellen Van der Holden," she said, holding out her hand for me to shake. I took it and smiled back at her. "It's such a pleasure to meet you. Your mother's told me many wonderful things."

I'm sure she has. "It's a pleasure to meet you as well." I waved my hand towards my friends. "These are my bridesmaids, Beatrice and Felicity Paxton. They're helping me out with some of the planning."

Everyone shook hands and Ellen led us back to the design room where the entire process evidently took place. Over the next two hours, we poured over books and catalogs, played with software on the computer, and relentlessly fiddled with a variety of materials, which were now spread out all over the table we were sitting at.

I was tired and I hated all of the designs. It wasn't poor Ellen's fault; I just didn't like the particular style she seemed to favor. It was all too ostentatious and a bit pompous. I mean, we weren't Will and Kate for crying out loud. Nobody was going to frame the freaking invitation to our wedding. I had to remember, though, that my mother chose this vendor, so it was no wonder that I wasn't a big fan of any of the designs. Beatrice and Felicity didn't seem too taken with any of them either, but time was winding down and I knew I needed to choose something to placate my mother. Plus, Ellen actually seemed very sweet and it wasn't her fault that my mother was a control freak, so I didn't want to upset her either.

I ended up choosing the one I hated the least and said goodbye to Ellen, who informed us that she should have the proof ready for me in two weeks. The girls seemed just as relieved to be out of there as I did by the time we exited the building and started walking in the direction of the caterer's storefront. Normally, we'd call one of our drivers, but the building was close enough for a walk and we'd probably be glad we did after we consumed the amount of the food waiting for us at Mediterranean Cuisine.

"Thank the good Lord we are out of there. I swear, if I had to look at anymore damn calligraphy and ugly ribbon, I was goin' to shoot somethin'," Beatrice complained as we walked along the sidewalk.

It really was a gorgeous day and it felt great to get some fresh air, as fresh as city air could be, anyway.

Felicity nodded her head in agreement while letting out an exasperated sigh. "I agree. Did you like any of those designs?" she asked me, her tone indicating that she already knew the answer.

I shook my head. "No, not really. But what can I do? My mother will get her way regardless so I might as well save us some trouble."

Beatrice stepped closer to me and put her arm around my shoulders. "Aw, honey," she murmured sympathetically.

They both understood my predicament but never knew what to say to help the situation. They tried in the past but had eventually figured out it was a moot point. Now, they were just there for me and that was all I could really hope for.

Another two hours later and I felt miserable. Satisfied and completely sated but miserable. The owner, Ramón, had had so many appetizers prepared that we hardly ate our entrées when he brought them out. Everything was to-die-for delicious and the girls seemed to think so, too. I was more than happy to handle this part of the planning, and Ramón certainly had my vote for catering the not-so-blessed event.

"So," Felicity began as she scooted back in her chair, done with her meal, and reaching for her wine glass, "how was the dinner last night?" Her earnest expression as she waited for my answer told me that she expected some juicy gossip.

I shrugged nonchalantly. "Same as always. William rubbed elbows with all the stuffed suits in attendance, while I had to endure one inane conversation after another with the hooligans of high society." I started absently running my finger along the rim of my wine glass as I spoke. "The chocolate fountain and trays of champagne were the only things that got me through it."

Felicity chuckled softly and nodded her head at me. "No way you can ever go wrong with a chocolate fountain."

"I heard the guy running against William was supposed to have been there. Did you meet him? What's his name, Masters or somethin' like that?" Beatrice was only giving the conversation half of her attention while she checked out the ass of a passing waiter, her eyebrows raising in obvious appreciation.

But my heart had stopped at the mention of Clay's name, and I suddenly had no clue what to say. My mind went completely blank. I could feel sweat start to gather on my forehead as I searched for words.

What the hell is wrong with me? All she did was say his name!

Her head popped up at my hesitation to answer, and her eyes narrowed in curiosity at the blush I could feel spreading across my face. I tried to stop it but couldn't help it. And now both of their interests were piqued.

Great.

"Okay, spill," Beatrice demanded.

"Nothing. I just met him, we talked for a few minutes and that was it. He was polite."

I couldn't make eye contact with them just yet. I had to get my thoughts under control and my blood pressure to stop rising every time I heard that man's name. We talked, that's all. It didn't mean anything. *Right?*

"He was polite," Beatrice slowly repeated, as if she were trying to dissect what I just said.

"Yes. He seemed nice." I hoped I sounded convincing. I didn't need to be thinking about him anymore than I already was. And I really didn't need them badgering me about it when even I couldn't explain my reaction to him.

"And I suppose he's not as gorgeous in real life as I've heard he is, huh?" she asked with a challenge in her voice, like she was daring me to correct her.

I wouldn't take the bait.

"What do you want me to say? Sure, he's obviously good-looking."

She didn't say anything but she still looked suspicious, obviously not buying my lackadaisical responses. Felicity had been sitting there, listening intently, but chimed in when she asked, "So, what did he say? What did you talk about?"

I shrugged again, doing my best to act apathetic to the conversation. "Nothing special. Literature, the campaign. It was only for a few minutes." *But it had felt a lot longer than that.*

"Then why are you blushing?" Beatrice questioned. She was too perceptive. She had always had a knack for reading people.

"I'm not blushing. It's just the wine. I always get flushed when I drink wine," I countered.

"Darlin', you're definitely blushing," Felicity said with a devious little smile on her button face. "It's okay, you know. You can think a man is handsome."

"Oh, please. I have a fiancé and he's running against Clay. I talked to the man for two minutes." I took a long swig of my wine, hoping that might calm my nerves. Thinking about him got me worked up in more ways than one. As if on cue, an image of Clay smiling at me appeared in my head, sending heat straight down to my womanly parts, forcing me to squeeze my thighs together.

Dammit. I chugged some more of my wine, hoping that might contain my sudden burst of arousal.

"A first name basis already? Interesting," Beatrice muttered. She wasn't even attempting to hide her all-knowing smirk.

"Don't you dare get that look on your face," I chided her. "Don't you go getting all these crazy ideas in your head. He's handsome, yes, but so are a lot of men. We had a brief conversation because he's running against my fiancé and he thought he'd introduce himself," I lied. He hadn't actually known who I was before he approached me, but they didn't need to know that.

Beatrice put her hands up in surrender. "Hey, you don't have to go defendin' yourself to me. I mean, it's not a crime to innocently flirt with a beautiful man. In fact, if he's as gorgeous as his pictures, flirting with *that* particular man could be a whole lot of fun." She winked at me as she drained the rest of her glass.

"Lord Almighty, Bea," Felicity exclaimed as she took a drink of her sweet tea. "Can't you keep it in your pants for at least a whole day?"

"Hey, I'm not the one who has a problem in her pants. That would be Gwen over here," she tilted her head towards me as she poured herself another glass.

"Oh, really? I'm the one with the problem, Miss 2-in-1-nighter?" I quipped.

Beatrice laughed but had the decency to blush. At the same time, Felicity groaned and pretended to gag as she said, "Ew, can we not? I was just beginning to forget hearing some of the details from that night. Let's not rehash it."

Although Felicity didn't like to think about it, I loved giving Bea crap about her drunken dirty dalliances with two, yes two, men in one night. Of course, they had been more than just dalliances. She had just graduated with her master's degree, and she wanted to, um, celebrate. And celebrate she did. She ended up screwing a guy in the bathroom at a club, and then took a *different* guy home with her at the end of the night. We both lectured her on how incredibly stupid it was, but she assured us that they'd been safe and she admitted that it was idiotic on her part and she would never do it again.

"It made for a good story, though, didn't it?" she smirked at us.

"I'd say more like disturbing," muttered Felicity.

I rolled my eyes at Bea but her earlier words stuck in my head. I *had* been flirting with Clay. I'd known it even at the time but I hadn't cared. Our banter had easily flowed between us, and it had been so nice and refreshing to talk to a man who hadn't known who I was at first and who made me forget for a minute how twisted my life had become. I suppose he could have lied about not knowing who I was but his surprise seemed genuine.

Yes, I'd flirted with him and enjoyed it. No, there wasn't anything really wrong with that, though William certainly would disagree.

Although, as Bea's words kept reverberating in my mind, I had to admit that my words and actions may have seemed innocent enough as I spoke to Clay, but the thoughts that had been running through my head since last night were anything *but* innocent.

Dammit. Now I was more aroused than ever.

Maybe chugging the wine wasn't such a good idea.

CHAPTER SIX

DISTRESS AND RESCUE

Gwen

Over a week later, my head was still a boggled mess, so I went for a run at my favorite park in the city. I didn't get the opportunity to run much anymore, as much as I would like to, but I took advantage when I could. Whereas writing helped take me to another world where I was able to vent my frustrations in an alternate reality, running cleared my head altogether. I didn't have to think or plan or put on a fake smile. I could just have a bit of peace for a moment and I felt rejuvenated afterwards.

It wasn't even nine o'clock yet, but the temperature this morning was particularly warm, so there were quite a few people at the park. Not wanting to bother Roberto this morning, I decided to drive myself and parked a block away, hoping I could easily get back out into traffic later.

As I walked towards the entrance to the park, I adjusted the strap that help my iPod on my arm and put my hair into a ponytail. The spandex running shorts and tank top I wore allowed for a lot of movement—I hated running in loose, baggy clothing. I started stretching my arms as I walked through the entrance, heading to a grassy area where I could finish stretching my legs before I took off on the trail that went around the perimeter of the park.

I couldn't help but watch the children play on the playground in front of me. Their smiling faces and exuberant laughter had me smiling and longing for a different life. One where I wasn't in the public eye and I was engaged to another man, one with a regular eight to five job, and we had a modest house in the suburbs with three kids. It probably sounded boring to some people, but that was everything that I'd never had. Compared to the life I had now, it seemed blissful.

For once, I just wanted normal.

Feeling stretched and warmed up, I took off at a brisk pace down the path, passing senior citizens playing chess and other runners taking advantage of the warm morning, while AC/DC. blasted through my headphones. I'd been running for maybe ten minutes when I felt someone tap me on the shoulder. I was so absorbed in the song I was listening to while trying to clear my head, my body jolted to the side, causing me to almost step off the path and fall face first into some bushes.

After I regained my balance, I looked over to see who was trying to get my attention and I almost lost my footing again.

Clay Masterson stood before me, in black athletic shorts and a plain white t-shirt, which clung to every one of his chest and arm muscles, causing my jaw to drop an embarrassing distance. I was basically drooling. The way the sun was hitting him in that moment made his tanned skin look like it was glowing. His midnight black hair had a shiny but mussed look to it, like he had just gotten out of bed, and it looked like perfection because this *man* was pure perfection. It was a look that only Clay could master.

Before I could stop myself, I licked my lips as I took in his body. *My God, I'm salivating at the mere sight of the man.*

Like a dog.

I *really* needed to get myself together.

To my utter humiliation, the man had a huge grin on his face as he took in my reaction to seeing him there. I couldn't blame him. I was making an ass out of myself. I was acting like I'd never seen an attractive man before.

"Well, hello Gwen McKindry," he said in that intoxicatingly deep voice, "what a surprise to see you here this morning."

I had to take a moment before I could speak because I was breathing so hard. And it wasn't from the running. "Mr. Masterson. It's good to see you again."

I gazed up into his bright blue eyes and felt more like I was falling into them. When he looked at me, I felt like he could see all of me, as if he knew all of my secrets and could see right through the armor I put up. That, of course, was just absurd, but his eyes were still assessing me intensely as I waited for his response.

"Call me Clay, please." His smile stayed on his face as he said this, but it seemed to be a warm and genuine one, rather than a polite grin that I would give to some random acquaintance. It made me feel good to think that he might look at me as something more.

I swallowed nervously. "Okay…Clay." I cleared my throat and tried to rein in my overactive hormones. "What are you doing here?"

Seriously? He's in running clothes, you idiot. What do you think he's doing here?

He didn't seemed to notice the stupidity of the question and just responded, "I come running here when I can. Clear my head, you know? My campaign office is only two blocks away, so it's convenient."

Right. His campaign office. He was running against my fiancé in the election. He was William's opponent. *Perspective, Gwen.*

"Oh, right." I didn't really know what else to say to that, but he saved me from any botched attempt at a subject change.

"Do you come running here a lot? I don't think I've ever seen you here before."

"I only come when I have time, which isn't that often these days. It's my favorite park, though, and it's never too crowded in the mornings."

I took in the scene around me, looking towards the path curving around the corner into the forested area up ahead. That was my favorite section of the park because it felt like you were miles and miles away from the city when you were completely surrounded by greenery.

He nodded his head in understanding and replied, "Yeah mine, too." He paused and seemed to be considering what he was about to say. "I'm not trying to sound weird or anything, but since we're both here, do you want to run together?"

He had such a sheepish look in his eyes as he asked the question, it pretty much made him irresistible. I couldn't say no. It felt like I'd be disappointing a little kid if I did. Which was probably really weird when you think about it. But running together was harmless. Right?

I smiled at him and said, "Sure, why not. Although, you're probably in much better shape than I am. I haven't ran in a while and when I do, it's usually at a snail's pace."

I said it as a joke, to keep things from feeling awkward, but when he didn't respond right away, I looked up at him. His earlier smile was gone and instead his lips were pulled into a tight line as his eyes traveled slowly up and down my body, pausing a little longer on certain places. I may not be the most experienced woman when it came to relationships, or really any kind of encounters with members of the opposite sex, but when he met my eyes again, there was no doubting the heat I recognized there. I saw glimpses of it that night when I first met him at the dinner, but now it was coming out full-force.

This man wanted me. Or at least, he liked what he saw.

"I highly doubt that you're in bad shape, Gwen. You put every other person running here to shame, including me." His voice had more of a rasp to it now and he was speaking slower than before, like he was putting more meaning behind his words.

Clay Masterson, a god among men, wanted me. Which was something I couldn't really wrap my mind around. I was doused with an overwhelming sense of pride at this realization. Even though nothing could come of it, I was satisfied knowing that a man like him could actually want a woman like me.

I chuckled softly and shook my head, as I took off once again at a steady pace, expecting him to follow. He did.

"And I doubt that you would have any trouble keeping up. You look like you work out seven days a week," I said without thinking.

I was immediately embarrassed and could feel my cheeks heat. *Shit, why had I said that?* I basically told him that I'd been checking him out. That I thought he looked good!

He didn't seem embarrassed, however, and simply laughed good-naturedly. "Usually just five days a week, depending on my work load. But thank you."

He looked over at me and gave a knowing grin. He knew damn well what I had meant and was enjoying my humiliation. I couldn't hate him for it, though. He was being cocky but in a non-arrogant way, if that made any sense. It was cute and I didn't want him to be cute, dammit.

I couldn't prevent the smile from forming on my lips. I muttered a "you're welcome" under my breath and focused on my running. I was starting to feel warmer and could feel the sweat gathering on my back, but I was sure it wasn't from the warm sun. The man running next to me was practically the match to my flame, lighting everything inside me on fire with just a heated look or a sexy smirk.

Who am I kidding? He could do it just by breathing.

We ran in companionable silence for several minutes before he spoke. I hadn't minded the quiet, though. It wasn't awkward at all like I would have expected. I realized that I was as comfortable running with him as I had been talking to him at the dinner. Probably not the best sign.

"So you like reading, running, and mocking high-ranking members of society. What else does Gwen McKindry enjoy?" he asked, as we entered the forested section. He didn't even sound the least bit winded. *Guess he wasn't kidding about that five days a week thing.*

The question took me by surprise and I wasn't sure how to respond. I wasn't expecting a conversation while running.

"Um, well. I like to write," I said between breaths.

Why had I said that *of all things?* I needed a freaking muzzle or something because I obviously could not keep myself from saying insane things today. I'd never told anyone about my writing. He may be easy to talk to but that didn't mean I needed to tell him my most private thoughts.

"Really?" he asked, sounding interested which surprised me. I didn't figure he would care. "What kind of things do you like to write?"

Should I tell him? I barely knew this man. Could I actually talk to him about something that I never shared with anyone? *Eh, what the hell.* I already told him this much, and I didn't think he was the type of person to run to the media with it or anything. It was completely crazy, but he made me feel at ease opening up to him.

"Well, I like to write suspense stories. Thrillers, sometimes horror. That sort of thing. I've actually written a few that are more like full-length novels." *Okay, that's enough word vomit. You don't have to go overboard here.*

"Wow," he remarked, sounding genuinely impressed. "That's awesome. Are you going to publish them?"

I should have expected that question. "Um, no, probably not. I mean, I doubt they're good enough for publication."

I could feel his eyes on me but I avoided them. I was afraid of what he might see in mine if I looked up. It sometimes felt like the man was a mind reader.

"You'll never know unless you try. It couldn't hurt to send them to someone and see, right?"

I tried to shrug, which probably looked really awkward since we were running, but I wanted to play it off like it didn't matter one way or another to me. Even though it did and I figured he would know it if I said too much.

"It's no big deal. I just write as a way to relax. It's not like I'd ever planned to make a career out of it or anything."

Again, I could feel his eyes on me and felt him wanting to say something—probably ready to call "bullshit" on me—but he remained silent.

Then he spoke up again after another minute. "Why thrillers and horror?" he asked in a more serious tone. *Too serious.* I wasn't about to divulge my deepest secrets to him. He may be the most beautiful man I'd ever seen, but I didn't strip myself bare like that for anyone.

We were coming up on a woman pushing a stroller in the middle of the path and we would have to split in order to go around her. I was about to give him a vague non-answer as we passed the woman when my foot slipped off the pavement and stepped right into a hole, twisting my ankle at an awkward angle and causing a sharp burst of pain to travel up my entire leg. I stumbled to the ground, crying out as I fell, and immediately grabbed my ankle, squeezing it as if that would provide some relief.

Son of a bitch, that hurt! And, of course, Alexander Skarsgård's black-haired lookalike had to be there to see the whole thing.

Just my luck.

Clay came rushing over to me as soon as I went down and grabbed my shoulders, his eyes examining my face and scanning over the rest of me with a mix of both concern and alertness.

"Are you okay?" His voice sounded worried as his attention was brought to my ankle where my hands were still grabbing it.

"Yeah, it's just my ankle. I think it might be sprained," I said through gritted teeth. I didn't want to sound weak and helpless, but I couldn't deny that it *hurt*.

He removed my hands and gently replaced them with his on my ankle, turning it from side to side. I may have been in pain but I couldn't ignore the fact that his hands were touching me and my body was certainly reacting to it. A huge bolt of electricity shot through me when his fingers touched my skin. Heat traveled from my ankle all the way to my head, making me feel a little light-headed. His fingers paused for a second and his feet shifted underneath him, readjusting himself, before he continued his examination. *Had he felt that, too?*

"I'm going to take off your shoe so I can see it better, okay?" he asked but started untying my shoe before I could answer.

His fingers were gentle as he slowly removed my shoe and pulled down my sock to get a better look. He let out a whistle when he saw the swollen lump that was already starting to turn purple.

"Looks like you're going to have one heck of a golf ball there. We need to get some ice on it and wrap it up. Come on," he said as he grabbed for my hands and started pulling me up.

"No, no. I'll be fine. I can drive myself home and get some ice when I get there."

I tried to take a step and put weight on my ankle and immediately regretted my decision. I hissed as more pain hit me and I stopped again, putting all my weight on my left foot. Clay reached for me again and wrapped one of my arms around his shoulders, pulling me into his side. I could feel the heat emanating from his body and could smell his shampoo.

Why does he have to smell good right now? Who smells good when they work out? Why can't he smell gross, like sweat or an entire men's locker room or something?

"See, you can't even walk on it. Come on, I'll help you to my car. We've got a first aid kit at the office, and I can help you wrap it and get some ice for it."

His office? As in, his campaign office? Yeah, that was definitely not a good idea. I shook my head and tried to get him to stop walking.

"Clay, I can't be seen going to your campaign office. Do you realize what that would look like if a reporter saw?" I couldn't believe he was being so cavalier about this. Did he not see what a monumentally bad idea this was?

He scoffed at my comment and started to walk again. "It's fine, Gwen. You're just hurt and I'm helping you. It's not a big deal."

I stopped walking again. "That's not how it will look, trust me. If the media can get even one picture, they could spin the story however they wanted. It's not even a good idea for us to be walking like this together."

I tried to remove his arm from around my waist, but he held it even tighter, not having any of it.

"Stop being difficult." I huffed indignantly at his words but he continued before I could say anything. "I'm not letting you leave this park alone with your ankle like that. We'll go in through the back door of the building. It's in an alley and isn't visible from the street. Will that work?"

I considered it for a minute. It still wasn't a good idea, but I knew I needed to get ice on my ankle and elevate it as soon as possible. And I really wanted to sit down.

I sighed and muttered, "Fine. Let's go."

I tightened my grip on his shoulder and let him drag me off to his car. I sent up a silent prayer that no one saw me holding onto a man who was not my fiancé while he helped me into his car right before we drove away together.

Alone.

This wasn't exactly what I had in mind when I wanted to go clear my head.

CHAPTER SEVEN

HEATED GAZES AND GENTLE GRAZES

Gwen

Ten minutes later, Clay was helping me out of his car and into the back door to the building of his campaign office. Luckily, his office was in the back so we didn't have to walk past his entire campaign staff, with him practically carrying me.

The drive had been excruciating but not because of the pain in my ankle. No, it was because Clay's entire car had smelled like *him*. Whatever spicy, woodsy scent it was that I had smelled on him the first night we met attacked my nose the moment I was inside that car. The whole ride my mind had drifted to thoughts of whether or not his bedroom would smell the same, especially his bed. That, of course, led to thoughts of how much clothing he liked to sleep in, which inevitably led to wondering what he would look like naked—spectacular, I was sure—which, obviously, led to questions of how the man would perform in bed. There was no doubt in my mind that he would know exactly what to do with a woman's body, and he would do it remarkably well.

I had been squirming so much in my seat trying to quell the ache between my legs that Clay probably thought I was in much more pain than I was. Well, I was in pain, just of a completely different nature than what he would have assumed.

He opened the door to an office that I assumed was his and sat me down on the brown leather sofa that sat against the back wall. He grabbed a throw pillow off of it and told me to lean back and prop my foot on top of the pillow while he went to grab the first-aid kit and some ice. I already missed the warmth of his body next to mine.

I was pretty pathetic.

With nothing else to do, I took in his office, with its beige walls and hardwood floors. There were two large wooden bookshelves against the wall in front of me, lined with books, binders, and a few picture frames that I couldn't see well from where I sat. His diplomas from the University of Virginia were hung on the wall behind his desk next to a photo of a younger Clay shaking hands with former President George W. Bush. On his desk sat piles of papers and folders, which would seem messy to most people, but they looked neatly stacked and organized. His desktop computer sat off to the side, and I could see another picture frame sat next to it. I was curious who that one was of since it had pride of place on his desk.

Oh my God. Something occurred to me right then that I hadn't considered before. *How stupid can I be?* He probably had a girlfriend. A man like him would most certainly be seeing someone, and that picture was probably of her and here I sat on his couch, waiting for him to come wrap my ankle. He was probably just pitying me, trying to be the gentleman by sweeping me up and bringing me back here to take care of me.

Of course, he wouldn't be doing all of this because he genuinely likes you. He knows you're engaged.

Suddenly, I felt sick to my stomach and unbearably humiliated. I sat up and started to swing my legs off the sofa to stand up and get the hell out of there when Clay walked back through the door, closing it behind him.

"What are you doing? I told you to keep it elevated or it's going to swell up even more," he said in a firm voice as he gently eased me back down onto the sofa.

"I really shouldn't be here. You've probably got a million things you need to do and I don't want to get you into any trouble."

He handed me a bottle of water and sat down on the end of the couch where my ankle was. He placed the first-aid kit next to my leg and took out the roll of athletic wrap.

"I already told you it was fine that you're here, and who would I get in trouble with?" he asked as he turned my ankle to the side so he could inspect the swelling.

I shifted my body around, embarrassed by the question. I didn't want to say it, but it needed to be said. "Um, your...ahh... girlfriend," I said it more like a statement than a question because he *had* to be dating someone. Men like him don't stay single for long.

At my words, Clay's hands abruptly stopped what they were doing and he looked over at me, directly into my eyes. He had a questioning look in his eyes but his jaw was tight and I could see his muscles clench.

"Who said I had a girlfriend?" he asked, seeming more curious than annoyed, which was a relief. I really wasn't trying to pry into his personal life. I just didn't want to cause any problems in it.

I nervously bit my lip and averted his eye contact, feeling a little shy under his scrutiny. "I just assumed you were seeing someone. I'm sorry, I wasn't trying to be nosy or anything."

I peeked up at him through my lashes and saw that he was still studying me. After another moment, his mouth formed into a smirk and he let out a short chuckle, as he shook his head.

"Nope, no girlfriend," was all he said.

I'm sure he saw the look of surprise that flashed on my face at his words. No girlfriend? How was that possible? Maybe he was the type of man who preferred to just date, or sleep, around and avoid commitment. Either way, the enormous sense of relief that flooded through me at this piece of information confused me more than I cared to acknowledge in that moment. So, I simply ignored it.

He placed a bag filled with ice that I hadn't even seen him carry in directly on my ankle, causing me to hiss as the temperature sent a chill through my body. His eyes flickered to my face and he murmured a sympathetic "sorry" as he began to roll the athletic wrap around the bag and my ankle with controlled expertise. It certainly looked like he'd done this before.

"Where did you learn how to do that?" I asked, suddenly wanting to know more about this man.

His eyes met mine briefly before returning to his task. "I played sports in high school, mainly baseball. Even played in college. So I've had my share of wrapping an ankle or two."

I couldn't say I was surprised that he was a talented athlete. He's obviously built for that type of physical activity. And, of course, my mind drifted to images of him in his baseball uniform, swinging a bat, running around the bases. God, he must have looked good in those tight pants. Like a lot of women, I could always appreciate a man in uniform, and I was sure that Clay would have attracted the opposite sex like moths to a flame while in his jersey. Not that he needed to be in uniform now to garner female attention because he didn't. He could be wearing a potato sack and still have hundreds of women swooning in his wake.

I tried to ignore the sparks that his fingers sent up my leg as he continued to guide the wrap around my swollen ankle. I took a deep breath, attempting to steer my thoughts in the opposite direction as I brought my attention back to our conversation. "What position did you play?"

"I was a pitcher. Starting pitcher all four years in college," he proudly added, but I could tell he wasn't trying to be arrogant about it.

"Did you like playing?" I asked. I had a sense that it was more to him than just a game. Couldn't tell you why I thought that, but I did.

He raised his head, meeting my eyes with a bright smile on his face. "I loved it. Some of the best years of my life," he said without hesitation.

"So, what made you quit? I mean, could you have played professionally? What made you choose politics?" *Holy crap, stop bombarding him with questions. You're probably annoying him.*

He didn't seem annoyed, though. Instead, he had a wistful look on his face as he considered my question. After a few moments he replied softly, "I probably could have went pro, but I didn't think it was for me. My heart was in public service, and I knew I'd have a longer career in that than I would in baseball. It wasn't a hard decision for me." He brought his eyes back to me, his blue irises boring through mine, and I could feel the tension starting to build in the room as our eyes stayed locked on each other.

Trying to keep the moment as much in the innocent zone as possible, I blinked my eyes, turning my head away from him and breaking the connection. Every nerve ending in my body desperately wanted to lean forward and touch him, but I resisted the urge as I cleared my throat and responded, "Well, it seemed like the right choice for you, then."

I could still feel his intent eyes on me as I twisted my hands in lap, refusing to look up at him until I got myself under control. Thankfully, he got back to work on my ankle and asked, "So, what about you? Did you play any sports growing up?"

My heart slammed painfully in my chest at his question. "Uh, no. My parents never allowed me to play any sports. Said I never had the time for them. The closest I got was horseback riding, which I loved. Though, I didn't get to do that as often as I would have liked, either," I said with regretful longing evident in my voice.

I used to beg my parents to let me play sports with the other kids when I was young, but they practically ignored my pleas every time. They'd said it would have been a waste of my time, and I needed to concentrate on my studies and more important extracurricular activities, like model UN or running for student council. They'd enrolled me in riding lessons for a couple of summers and I'd loved it. Though, they could sense I was getting too attached to it when I started asking to go riding all hours of the day, and that was when they stopped the lessons and forced me to concentrate on something more useful, like the debate team.

I'd been devastated, of course. Horseback riding had offered a certain freedom to me that I couldn't find anywhere else in my life at that age and they coldheartedly stole it away from me. I think that was when my contempt for my parents really started to culminate.

Clay could apparently sense the enmity behind my words because he paused his movements again, laying his hand on my knee in a comforting gesture. It was doing anything but comforting me, though. It sent jolts of lightning up my leg right to the sensitive area between my thighs, scorching every inch of skin along the way. "I'm sorry," he said. *What is he sorry about? What are we even talking about?* I couldn't remember, couldn't think properly when he touched me like that. "That must have been tough. It doesn't sound like you had a very fun childhood." *Right, we were discussing the thrilling details of my dreary background.*

I released a sarcastic laugh at his words, which he must have assumed meant that I was offended because he said, "Sorry, I wasn't trying to be rude or imply that—"

I held up my hand to stop him before he could say anything else. "Please, no, don't worry about it. I wasn't upset or anything. You're right. It wasn't a very fun childhood. My parents always kept me busy without offering me much say in the matter, and I more or less had all of my decisions made for me. It wasn't always easy growing up in the McKindry family," I said flatly. I shouldn't be talking about this with him. I was sure he didn't want to hear me whine about my unfortunate upbringing as a spoiled, rich kid.

"I can't imagine. Hopefully, things got better as you got older?" he said, phrasing it as more of a question than a statement. His voice was prompting and he actually sounded interested in getting more information from me. His facial expression was earnest but pensive, his eyes inquisitive as he waited for my answer, which was something new. I didn't usually have someone around to just *listen* to me like this. It was nice.

"Um, sort of," I stammered. How to explain my family? I didn't exactly want to air out our dirty laundry to him because it wasn't pleasant and I didn't want his pity. "Let's just say it was complicated being under constant public scrutiny like that, and my parents didn't always understand how to separate it from our home life. They still don't." *Crap.* That was probably revealing too much. I was really starting to get uncomfortable with this conversation.

As always, Clay seemed to read my mind, nodding his head and saying in a low voice, "I understand that. Well, I'm sorry you had to go through that, Gwen."

He looked like he wanted to say more, but instead, he went back to wrapping my ankle in silence as I tried to block out the feelings of melancholy threatening to overtake my mood. Thoughts of my parents and memories of my past always brought about rancorous emotions for me and I hated it. I didn't want those people and their poor childrearing methods to continue to bring me down even in my adulthood. I was so sick of them having such a strong effect on my life. To be honest, I was sick of even having them in my life at all.

As I focused back on the present and the sight before me, lust slowly began to curl around my body, consuming my thoughts and igniting all my sexual urges. If there was one person in the world who could drag me out of my surly descent into misery, it was the beautiful man in front of me.

His hands accomplished the task of wrapping my ankle with smooth, dexterous movements, drawing my thoughts back to his bedroom activities. *Oh, what his hands could probably do to me.* The familiar ache between my legs started building once again as I pictured those hands traveling up my thighs, spreading them right here on this sofa, while his fingers inched up, closer and closer to my most sensitive area. His warm breath on my neck as he left a trail of hot, wet kisses down to the top of my breasts. He'd drag down my tank top with his teeth, leaving my breasts exposed to his lascivious mouth, his tongue tracing my puckered nipple before taking the entire thing in his mouth, sucking deep and hard. He'd press his hard body against me as he brought his mouth back up to take mine in a soul-searing kiss as he slammed his hips into mine, grinding his hardened length against my sex. His fingers would slide underneath my pants, shoving my panties aside and slowly start to rub my—

"All done," Clay announced all of sudden, breaking me out of my X-rated and completely inappropriate thoughts. I realized that I was breathing harder and my body felt like it was on fire.

Geez, where had all of that come from? I must be about to start my period, or maybe I have a hormonal imbalance or something.

Clay looked up at me when I didn't respond and seemed to sense something in my eyes because he stopped what he was doing and locked his eyes with mine. Neither one of us broke eye contact or moved a muscle. The room was utterly silent, except for both our breathing, his starting to come faster and harsher. I could see his hands clenched into fists in front of him, and his eyes left mine for a moment as they moved down my body in the most sensual perusal I'd ever experienced. I could feel that look in my heart, my stomach, below my waist, and even in my toes. It was *that* powerful.

That look said everything that we couldn't. It said *I want you.* It said *I'd take you right now if I could.* It said *I've never craved anything more in my life than you right here, right now.*

At least, that's what it felt like to me. I hoped my eyes were saying the same things. I needed him to understand that I wanted those same things, craved those same things. His eyes came back up to mine. Their color had changed to a darker blue as they dilated with lust and need and so much heat that nothing short of an ice cold bath would cool me down after this.

I licked my lips as I took in his gorgeous body. His eyes widened slightly at the movement and his breathing increased. We were both practically panting now. He shifted his body around as he began to inch farther up, closer to me. He placed his hands on the couch along both sides of my body, and without thinking, I spread my legs to give him more room.

His knee shifted between my legs as he brought his chest right up against mine, bringing his face at eye level with me. We never broke eye contact as he moved up the sofa and I was sure my heart was about to beat out of my chest. I didn't know what to do with my hands—I was afraid if I touched him, I wouldn't be able to stop—so I kept them at my sides, gripping the couch so hard my knuckles were turning white.

One of his hands was now braced near my head, against the arm of the couch and the other one was placed on the couch by my waist, keeping his body propped up above mine. He kept space in between our lower halves—probably a good idea—but our chests were lightly rubbing together. I was sure he could feel my puckered nipples through the thin material of our shirts. My suspicion was quickly confirmed a second later when his forehead creased as if he was in pain, closing his eyes briefly as let out a short moan.

He opened his eyes again and met mine, but the crease in his forehead didn't go away, and the look in his eyes was now a mixture of heat and desperation. Our faces were but inches apart. It would have been so easy to just reach up, grab the back of his head, and bring his lips crashing down onto mine but I waited to see what he would do.

His head started moving slowly towards mine, while at the same time his mouth opened like he was about to say something. But before anything could happen, a loud shrill rang through the room, cutting through the tension and silence like the sharpest butcher knife.

He slammed his eyes shut and sighed as he dropped his head and said, "It's mine. I should probably get that."

Taking in a few deep breaths and trying to get my body under control, I nodded my head and said, "Yeah. I should get going anyway."

But he made no move to answer the phone and let it keep ringing, still staring at me. "I can drive you back to your car," he offered.

I immediately protested that idea. I had no clue what would happen if I spent any more time alone with this man. We both needed some space to calm down.

"No, that's not necessary. I'll call my driver, and he can be here in a few minutes." I didn't really know if it would only be a few minutes, but I had to get away from Clay before I did something truly desperate.

Like rip off my clothes and beg him to take me on this sofa.

He looked like he wanted to argue but stopped himself. "Okay. You can wait in here until he gets here."

That definitely wasn't happening either.

"No, I'll just wait out in the alley for him. Thanks a lot for helping me out. I really appreciate it." I knew I was talking fast and probably looked like an idiot trying to hobble out of that room as quickly as I could, but I didn't care. I was almost out the door when he spoke up.

"Gwen, I—" he started, but was interrupted by his phone ringing again.

Before he could say anything else because I was afraid of what he was going to say, I blurted out, "You'd better get that. I'll see you later, Clay."

With that, I was out of that door, down the hall, and out the back door before I even gave myself a chance to look back.

I limped into the alley, leaned against the damp brick wall, and tried to control my rapid breathing. I attempted to regulate my thought processes, but I couldn't establish any sense of order because only one question was flashing in bright neon lights in my head.

What the hell just happened?

Clay

Holy shit.

What the hell just happened?

I almost kissed Gwen McKindry. In fact, if I had kissed her I was damn sure I would have been tempted to do a *lot* more than that.

What the hell was I thinking? She's engaged and I don't want or need that kind of trouble in my life. Thank God my phone rang. I didn't even care who it was. I didn't answer it after she left my office. I couldn't concentrate on anything other than how she had felt underneath me, so there was no way I was answering a phone or talking to any human being until I got myself, and every hard and very aroused part of me, under control.

I had no idea what had come over me, but when she had looked at me with *that* look—that look that practically invited me to slam her back into the sofa and take her so damn hard she screamed in blissful pleasure—well, I sort of lost it. I mean, the woman had licked her lips like I was her next meal. What was a man supposed to do?

Even before I saw that look in her eyes, I knew what thoughts had been running through her head. Her body had shivered when I was wrapping her ankle. She was squirming around on that couch and squeezing her legs together as if seeking some relief. I knew she'd been getting hot and had started sweating because she kept rubbing her hands on those hot spandex shorts. I don't even think she realized when she had started to breathe faster.

But I noticed.

Oh man, had I noticed.

As worked up as she'd been getting, I'd been even worse. I was hard the minute I'd seen her in the park and the situation hadn't improved after that. I'm sure she felt she same jolt of electricity that I'd felt whenever we touched. And I hoped that I'd covered the tent in my shorts but after a while, there was no hiding it. I had to readjust myself so many times in the car on the way to the office because I'd looked over to her side only once and saw her hardened nipples—damn air conditioner—through her thin tank top and then the situation in my shorts became painful.

I didn't look over at her again.

It didn't matter, though, because I was on full alert by the time I started wrapping Gwen's ankle. The feel of her soft, smooth skin beneath my fingers elicited images of what the rest of her body would look and *feel* like. Her scent—whether it was shampoo or lotion or perfume, I didn't know—had surrounded me and was the most intoxicating combination of sweet and citrus I'd ever smelled. And whenever she spoke, her voice was like honey, the sexiest sound that had ever reached my ears.

And when she'd been talking about her family and her childhood, all I'd wanted to do was wrap my arms around her and comfort her. She'd insinuated that she was still having to deal with her parents and their controlling ways, and that just pissed me off to no end. If that was the case, it would definitely explain the sorrow I could often feel in her and her aversion to living among the D.C. elite. When I saw the heartache in her eyes, my protective instincts had started to go into overdrive. I'd just wanted to hold her, hide her away from the rest of the world and tell her that everything was going to be okay.

In those moments, I didn't think about the fact that she had a fiancé and the man was my opponent. I didn't think about how it wasn't the right time in my life to start a new relationship. Because we couldn't really have a relationship anyway, right? And I sure as hell didn't care that the whole situation could bring a media shit storm down on both of us if anything happened.

All I had cared about was that we were alone, in my office, and on a sofa.

And I was touching her.

I had been desperate to feel her, taste her, *possess* her. I just wanted to *have* that woman and it was the strangest feeling. I didn't get possessive over women and I never had a desire to claim any of them. But this one was wreaking all kinds of havoc on my normal modes of operation. All the rules went out the window when I was around her and none of it made sense. This one woman was under my skin and was starting to take over every part of me.

I found myself thinking about her all the time, even while I was trying to work, which definitely wasn't a good sign. I thought back to our first conversation at the Stars and Stripes dinner and realized that I liked talking to her like that. Like two people who shared the same interests and seemed to enjoy each other's company. Of course, that was before I realized that she was engaged to my competition.

Still, though, I wanted to *talk* to her, to learn more about her. She was the most intriguing woman I'd ever met, and being around her was starting to feel more and more necessary. Like I was starting to suffocate the longer I wasn't around her and the only thing that could breathe life back into me was her.

And she's taken.

That was the reminder I needed. I had to quit acting like a love-struck teenager because that was not what this was at all. This was me lusting after an attractive woman. Period. She had a fiancé and I had a job to do. End of story.

With a resigned sigh, I headed to my private bathroom. I had to take care of some business if I was going to have even a prayer of getting any work done today.

And I knew exactly what I was going to be thinking about the whole time. Or rather, *who* I was going to be thinking about.

This was *definitely* not good.

CHAPTER EIGHT

PINK CHAMPAGNE AND GARDEN GETAWAYS

Gwen

The 5th annual charity luncheon for underprivileged youth, hosted by the conglomerate of youth centers in the D.C. area, was one of my favorite events every year. Admittedly, I typically hated most of the events that I was forced to attend. There were too many uptight, pretentious politicians and pseudo-philanthropists who showed up simply to throw their power and money around. And even though I'd been born into this lifestyle, I always felt like I didn't belong, like an outsider.

But this luncheon provided for a whole different set of characters. The majority of attendees were people who were involved in this type of work for the right reasons and had a passion for helping kids. I looked forward to hearing about the progress at the organizations and facilities around the city that did everything from providing shelter for the youth living on the streets to after-school tutoring. It meant a great deal to me to be able to help these groups in any way that I could.

Plus, this was also one of the few events that William never accompanied me to.

This year's luncheon was held at the Botanical Gardens. It was a beautiful, sunny Saturday afternoon and the conservatory and all of its landscaping splendor was a spectacular sight to behold.

I had on a chiffon halter dress with a floral print that tightly hugged my curves but showed off my figure in a modest way. The skirt was flowy and stopped just above my knees. I paired it with brown wedge sandals, gold hoop earrings, and light makeup and left my hair down in loose waves.

I was able to get a little bit of sun the day before when I laid by the pool, so I was pleased with the slightly golden tone of my skin. And some of the male attention I was receiving didn't escape my attention either. That didn't happen often since William was by my side most of the time and he doesn't take kindly to men ogling me. So, yes, I'll admit that it felt good seeing the looks of appreciation on these men's faces.

I mingled around the room, sipping on my glass of pink champagne as I went, and was introduced to many new faces. Some I committed to memory, some I forgot the second I turned away from them. I could recognize the smarmy types who were just there for a tax deduction when I saw them.

When it was announced that lunch was about to be served, I decided to take a bathroom break before I sat down. The bathrooms were located on the other side of the lobby and down a maze-like hallway. I went down a few dead ends and had to back track a couple of times. It ended up taking me almost ten minutes just to find them. Seriously, they needed signs.

I was looking down, smoothing out the skirt of my dress as I was coming out of the bathroom, when I ran into a brick wall that made me stumble backwards and almost fall on my ass. Luckily, two strong hands caught my arms and held me upright before I could embarrass myself in epic fashion.

I looked up and several things happened at once. My heart stopped, my breath hitched, my pulse rocketed to unhealthy levels, and my body did that whole thing where it heated up so fast and so hot that I felt like I had stepped into a sauna.

The most gorgeous face I'd ever seen was inches away from my own, smiling down at me. Blue eyes, sinful mouth, perfect teeth, and *dimples*.

Clay Masterson.

Of course this would happen to me. I felt like I was being taunted by the universe, having this beautiful man dangled in front of me, knowing full well that I couldn't do anything about it. Life is *so* not fair.

"Whoa, you okay?" His hands were burning holes into my arms but those marks I would certainly welcome.

"I—um, yeah I'm fine. Thanks. That could have been embarrassing." I thought I might be having a heart attack because the stupid muscle was beating so erratically and I couldn't get it to calm down.

A smile lit up his face, reaching all the way to his eyes. "Well, hello Gwen McKindry. It's nice to see you again."

Good Lord, he was devastating to look at, especially with his dimples staring me right in the face. I'd never had a dimple fetish before but I could definitely see the appeal.

"It's nice to see you too."

He let go of me and I immediately missed the warmth of his hands and wanted them back on me. I liked him touching me far too much. His eyes lazily roamed down my body, apparently not caring about how obvious he made it. When he met my eyes again I wasn't surprised this time to see the lust in them. After what happened the last time we were around each other, I was learning to expect the unexpected with this man. Images of that afternoon flooded my mind and I fought with every ounce of strength I had to ignore them.

I could not think of that right now or I would most definitely make a fool of myself. I could already feel my face heating with color.

"You look beautiful today," he said in a sincere but almost amused tone. He had to know by now how he affected me if the color of my face was any indication.

Though, I flushed an even deeper scarlet at his compliment. I just couldn't help it. As sad as it was, I wasn't used to compliments from men. Or anyone, for that matter. Beatrice and Felicity were the only people that I could actually count on to make me feel good about myself. Clay had sounded appreciative and for some reason, it mattered immensely to me that he liked what he saw. I honestly didn't know when the last time a man had said that to me and meant it. It certainly hadn't been by my fiancé. The fact that Clay said it made my insides twist and the rest of my body feel like mush. It was a strange sensation.

"Thank you." I nervously twisted my hands together in front of me, worried I was going to say the wrong thing and sound like an idiot.

"How is your ankle?" he asked, looking down at my foot and sounding genuinely concerned.

"Oh, it's much better, thank you. The swelling went down and it doesn't really hurt anymore."

I'd almost forgotten that I even hurt it. All semblance of thought disappeared every time I was around this man. In fact, I'd only kept it wrapped for a few days and iced it a couple of times after the day in his office. I limped everywhere those first couple days, and then the pain stopped. William had barely even noticed. All he did was ask me what happened in a disinterested voice and barely mumbled a response when I told him. I was able to keep Clay out of the story, *thank God*, by saying that I'd been able to make it back to my car and drive myself home. He hadn't asked about it again after that.

He smiled and said, "Good. I'm glad it healed quickly. It looked pretty painful in my office."

There it is. He went there. He mentioned that intense moment we had on the sofa where we almost…something. Kissed, I think? Either way, something had transpired between us, and I knew for a fact that he felt it too. His eyes had said it all and the look in them now said the same thing.

And his body right now was a little too close for comfort. Well, my body was very comfortable in such close proximity with this Greek god, but my head wasn't and I reminded myself that that was the part I had to listen to. Not the apparent carnal reaction I was having, always seemed to be having around him.

We began to walk back towards the conservatory in a comfortable silence. I was amazed at how easy it always was to be around him. He just seemed to exude a level of confidence that was strangely soothing. There was a quality of protectiveness and security in his mere presence that made me feel safe and at ease. Maybe I had a hero complex because he came to my rescue when I was injured but it felt like it was more than that.

"Is your fiancé here as well? I didn't think I saw him around."

My libido cooled down a little at the mention of William and I once again felt in control of my faculties. "No, he's not. He had some other pressing matters to attend to," I lied. I wouldn't be talking to Clay now if he were here, not after his reaction the night of our first encounter. I wasn't more grateful for his absence than I was in that moment.

Clay brought his eyes to mine, tilting his head as if considering something. "I see. Well that's too bad. I was hoping to discuss a few things with him. I'll have to catch up with him later, I suppose."

I knew they were opponents and would have to be around each other eventually, but I was surprised that Clay would want to speak with him one-on-one before all the campaigning began. I didn't understand why because it wasn't entirely necessary at this point, but I wasn't going to worry about it, or at least try not to.

I wouldn't lie and say that those two being alone in a room together didn't freak me out a little. There had been a noticeably strong undercurrent between the two of them at the Stars and Stripes dinner when they introduced themselves. There had been so much tension that I had even started to sweat as I witnessed the exchange.

Clay and I hadn't actually done anything more than talk but I still felt guilty for the feelings I had towards him. I figured Clay was feeling it too and I worried that he would somehow give something away to William, or perhaps antagonize him somehow, which would just piss him off and make him hate Clay even more. That anger, in turn, could eventually fall back on me.

We had stopped inside the entrance to the conservatory and turned to face each other as he continued to look at me with those intense eyes of his. An intensity that didn't frighten me like William's did but instead excited me. This *man*, I realized not for the first time, excited me.

Before I could take another step inside the room, he grabbed my elbow and asked, "Would you like to take a walk with me out in the gardens before we go back in?" He kept his eyes locked with mine the entire time he spoke. "It's really nice out there, if you haven't seen it."

Oh, boy. That doesn't sound like such a good idea. I was gripping my hands together so hard in front of me that I was starting to lose blood flow to them. I had been out to the gardens before and I loved it. It was charming, whimsical, *romantic.* And romantic was not good. "That's probably not such a good idea. I should really get back in there."

His hand left my elbow to reach out and gently grab my entwined hands, covering both of mine in one of his. And I could not for the life of me look away from his bright baby blues. "Please." He almost sounded like he was pleading. "Just for a minute."

If we hadn't been completely hidden by a huge plant right then, I would have yanked my hands back because it probably looked way too intimate. And it was, it definitely was.

Every fiber of my being was screaming at me to tell him "no" and run for the hills. Or at least run back into the conservatory where there were witnesses who could hold me accountable for my actions, prevent me from doing something irreversibly stupid, which I surely would if I was alone with this man.

But with him looking at me with such a hopeful, earnest expression, not to mention the way his warm hand was starting to caress both of mine, I knew I wasn't going to say no. As wrong as it probably was, for once in my life, I wanted to give in to what this man made me feel. I wanted to revel in it, if just for a moment. I knew it sounded cliché, but I wanted to feel *alive* and that's exactly how he made me feel every time I was around him. *Alive.*

And I only had so much will power.

I slowly nodded my head. "Okay."

Relief relaxed his face and, with a hand at the small of my back, he led me down a separate corridor and through a door that led to the garden at the back of the sprawling estate. There was a beautiful sparkling fountain cocooned in the middle of a garden utopia with a vast array of colors and textures that looked like a fantasy land. Like a place that only existed in fairy tales, or in dreams.

We walked along the cobblestone path that weaved through the peaceful Eden, and I was fully aware of how close our bodies were. I could feel his body heat, my own body being drawn to it as if his were physically reaching out for mine and pulling me closer.

"I love coming out here," he said in a calm, soothing voice that I wanted to melt under, "it's peaceful."

"It's lovely," I agreed, feeling wonderfully peaceful myself but anxious at the same time. I had no clue what his motivation was for bringing me out here. Well, I had some clue but I wasn't going to jump to conclusions.

"I agree." His voice took on a lower, huskier quality than just a second ago, like perhaps he was talking about more than just the garden, causing my head to shoot up and assess his expression.

He was looking right at me and stopped walking in the middle of the path. He made no move toward me but looked like he might be restraining himself. I didn't like that look or where his mind could be heading so I started walking again, hoping he followed. I heard his footsteps behind me a second later and I decided to change the subject to something less personal.

"So, what did you need to discuss with William?"

That's great. Switch to the topic of your fiancé. He'll surely love that.

He put his hands in his pockets and lifted his shoulder in a shrug. "Not much, I guess. Just wanted us to get better acquainted, so to speak. I mean, there's really no longer a need for formalities with us being mortal enemies and all."

I chuckled. "I think mortal enemies is a little strong. Don't you think there's such a thing as friendly competition?" I knew that with William there certainly wasn't. But I'd like to think there can be.

"In politics? Are you kidding me?" He looked at me with a mock look of horror and I let some of the tension leave my shoulders, appreciating his effort to lighten the mood.

"Okay, well maybe not friendly. But it doesn't always have to be hostile is my point."

"Well, when you're surrounded by sharks and lions one tends to become hostile."

I was slightly taken aback by that. "That's an interesting comparison to make. Those two don't even live in the same environment."

I found myself leaning closer to him, as if I could hurry his thoughts along, intrigued and wanting to hear what he would say next. "That's true, but see, they're both predators, preying on the weak at the first sign of fear. They're both fast and lethal when they attack. And they're both proprietary to a fault, destroying anything that encroaches on their territory, or anything that they consider theirs."

He took a step toward me as he made the last statement, his eyes penetrating mine. Suddenly, I had a feeling that we may not have been talking about politics anymore. Competition, maybe, but not politics. This wasn't the direction I needed this conversation to go. It was feeling way too intimate, but I couldn't stop myself from playing along. "I've found that politicians aren't much different," he added.

"So which one are you? The shark or the lion?" I forced myself to stay my ground. I felt brave and confident around this man for some reason, empowered even. I wanted to keep that feeling for as long as I could.

"Neither. See, the lion is the king of the jungle. But the problem is that there aren't enough kingdoms for all the lions in our jungle but everyone wants the title." I guess that was true. Power and entitlement meant everything to some of these people. "I don't want to rule, though. I just want to lead."

Even though it was a strange metaphor, I was moved at the impassioned speech and what was even more baffling, I absolutely understood what he meant. "And what about the others? The sharks," I asked with a slight smirk.

"Eh, the sharks are just the ugly ones," he quipped without any hesitation.

I burst into laughter and put my hand to my mouth, worried I'd draw attention to us. He smiled back at me, appearing smug and satisfied that he'd made me laugh. "Okay, well since you said you were neither, I guess I'm safe."

His longer than normal pause made me look up and meet his eyes again. "Who said you were?" He said it in such a sexy, breathy voice that I could feel my stomach muscles tighten as soon as it reached my ears.

Everything went incredibly still right then. Had he actually just said that, or was it my imagination?

The silence hung in the air between us, electrifying the space with so much sexual tension, I didn't want to even breathe for fear of breaking the connection. There was so much heat radiating throughout my body, I could feel the top of my head tingling, like some of it had to escape or I might explode.

As I stared back into his eyes, unable to look away even though I knew I should, I saw them darken, his pupils dilate, and jaw clench all at the same time. Again, his reaction was unlike William's because even though I didn't know this man well, I knew there was no violence behind those eyes. I was witnessing lust and desire transforming his face, not fury and aggression.

His jaw ticked as he continued to stare down at me, as if he was struggling to contain himself. From touching me, from saying something he shouldn't? I didn't know. But just for a moment I wanted to see him unleash that control on me and feel every bit of the passion emanating from his eyes. Experience the raw power and strength his hard, muscled body exhibited.

Time slowed down and I tried to think of something to say but couldn't come up with anything. I could think of a million things that I wanted to *do* and they all involved joining certain parts of our anatomies in the most filthy and inappropriate ways.

Inappropriate. Right. Just him standing so close was inappropriate. I needed to put some distance between us before someone saw and got the wrong idea.

I put my hands on his chest and gently shoved him away, stepping to the side, away from the wall. I cleared my throat and didn't want to meet his eyes, fearing what I might see there. That I might *like* what I'd see there. "I-I should, um, get back."

Yeah, even I could admit that I didn't sound too sure. *Quit stuttering, you idiot. You never stutter.*

He seemed to pick up on my uncertainty and said with a little bit of urgency in his voice, "Don't leave yet. Please. Just a few more minutes."

That *please* did it. Fine, just a few more minutes, but I was going to shift the conversation into safer territory. I started walking us down the path again, looking everywhere but at his face.

"I didn't expect to see you here today."

He seemed to relax a little at this, his shoulders slumping as if he were releasing some built-up tension there, his face clearing of whatever emotion had just overtaken it. "Don't tell me you're disappointed. I might be a little hurt by that." He gave me his best puppy dog eyes, seeming to share in my need to make light of the moment.

I smiled and gave a quick laugh. "Not at all, you just surprised me. I didn't realize you were involved in these types of charities."

He shrugged. "Not many people do. I try to keep my involvement with them out of the media as much as possible. I don't do it for the attention and I don't like to make a show of it."

My heart melted. "I can understand that," I said, nodding my head, "the media sensationalizes the notion of giving to charity too much, to the point where it stops becoming about the real needs of the recipients and more about the 'generosity' of the benefactors."

He smirked, recognizing the hint of sarcasm in my tone. "Are you saying not everyone is here out of the goodness of their hearts?" he asked, feigning bewilderment, "that the rich and powerful aren't all good people deep down and only want to help out their fellow man?"

I looked at him with raised eyebrows and scoffed in amusement. "I wish that were the case. With all human beings, really, not just the affluent."

I liked that even in his profession he didn't take himself too seriously. He liked to joke and be sarcastic and was just so grounded. At least with me, he didn't sugarcoat what he said and wasn't worried about it being splashed all over the front page of *The Washington Post* the next day. I liked that he seemed to feel as comfortable with me and I did with him.

"In a perfect world, right?" His eyes pierced through mine again, his voice taking on a more serious tone than it had a moment ago. My pulse spiked at both his words and the look in his eyes. I worked to slow the thumping in my chest before I braved a response.

"In a *decent* world." I met his gaze for a few consuming seconds before looking away and nervously twisting my hands in front of me again.

"Do I make you nervous, Gwen?" he asked suddenly, completely taking me aback with his bluntness.

"Why would you think that?" I was worried my voice betrayed my nerves, which he most assuredly had an effect on. Hell yes, he made me nervous, but in the most thrilling way possible.

He tipped his head down at my hands and replied, "You do that when you seem nervous. At least, I hope it's because you're nervous and not uncomfortable. You do it a lot around me and I don't want to make you uncomfortable." He stopped on the path again while he said this and faced me, arresting me in front of him with his soul-piercing eyes.

"No, I'm not uncomfortable around you. Just the opposite, in fact."

I probably shouldn't have said that but I abhorred the thought of lying to him. I couldn't explain it but it just felt wrong to do.

Something sparked in his eyes at my words, his expression snapping with some apparent conclusion he'd come to. He pulled his hands out his pockets, one of them taking hold of my wrist and pulling me off the path through a vine-covered archway that led to a small nook which wasn't visible from the path. The space was just big enough for two people and was surrounded by walls of green hedges with a roof of vines over our heads.

Basically, we were hidden away from the entire world right then, with no one to see or hear anything we were doing. My heart rate picked up to triple time its normal rate and I was sure I was seconds away from suffering a full-blown heart attack.

"Clay, what are you doing?" My voice was equal parts breathless and panic-riddled.

He pushed his body against mine until my back was pressed up against the hedge. One of his arms moved to my hip while the other he placed on the hedge near my head. He brought his face closer to mine until we were only inches apart, just like he had on the sofa in his office. Only this time there wasn't a door to separate us from the rest of the world. Nothing was stopping someone from walking through that archway and catching us.

But oh, his body feels good.

"I know you feel this too, Gwen." It sounded like a whisper and a groan at the same time. "I know you feel this connection between us. I'm not imagining anything, and you can't fake your reaction to me." His pupils had gotten even bigger and he was looking at me like he wanted to devour me. Strip me bare and eat me alive right here in the garden. And the crazy part was, I wanted to let him. *Oh God,* how I wanted him to do all those things to me and more.

Not giving into those desires was ripping my heart into pieces but I couldn't do this with him. It would be career suicide for him and just plain suicide for me if William were to find out. "I'm engaged, Clay. We can't do this, you know that."

"I know," he sighed heavily, "I know and I'm sorry." He hung his head and cursed himself under his breath. "I know I shouldn't be doing this, but I can't help it. I can't stop thinking about you and I can't be this close to you anymore without touching you. It's driving me crazy." Both of his hands came up and gently cupped my face, his own face was contorted in what looked like a heady combination of desperation, pain and need.

I reached up and grabbed both of his wrists and tried to wrench them away but he held tight. "This is way too dangerous, Clay. You don't even know how bad it would be if we were caught. It *can't* happen."

Now I was getting desperate myself as I pleaded with him, fighting back tears that were stinging my eyes. I had never fought with myself so much before in my life. I wanted him so bad the emotions were overwhelming but I had to protect him. If something happened and William found out, I had no doubts about the lengths he would go to make both of us pay. He had threatened my reputation and livelihood many times and I believed he would follow through on all of his promises if pushed. And I would never forgive myself if anything happened to Clay or his career because of me.

"It can if we want it to," he said adamantly as I started shaking my head at his words. "Yes, it can, listen to me. If we both want it bad enough, we can figure everything out. And I want it bad, Gwen." His hold on me tightened and he gently shook me as he continued softly, "I want you so much it's killing me. I want to be around you all the damn time and I hate that I can't be. I'm drawn to you in a way that I've never experienced with anyone and I can't ignore it anymore."

Every word was filling my heart with so much hope but breaking it at the same time because I knew that hope was just an illusion. "You don't know what he would do if he found out." My voice was shaky and my body was starting to tremble but I couldn't control it. "You don't understand how he is."

He dropped his hands and stepped back, thrusting both hands through his hair and breathing heavily. "I don't care about him! Dammit, Gwen, he's an asshole! You know that!" He looked back up at me with lust and anger in his eyes, his jaw clenching in frustration. When he spoke of William, he looked menacing which only served to turn me on even more and that, of course, made absolutely no sense.

I couldn't say anything to that. Of course, I knew he was an asshole, but Clay didn't really know how big of one and I wasn't about to tell him. I honestly didn't know how Clay would react if he found out that William had raised his hand to me, but I knew it wouldn't be pleasant. If I knew him as well as I thought I did, I figured that he'd most likely get angry and be tempted to confront William the next time he saw him, which would be the worst possible thing he could do. The worst thing for me, anyway. Somehow, I just knew that he couldn't find out the true nature of mine and William's relationship.

I loved the idea of having a knight in shining armor, but it didn't mean that I wanted him to get scorched by the dragon either.

He stood in front of me with his hands on his hips, looking up at the sky as if he were trying to rein in his frustration. He looked back at me, dead in the eyes, and asked, "Do you feel the same way about me?"

"It doesn't matter." I tried to look away but he started walking back towards me, trapping me in his gaze.

"It does to me. I need to know if you feel this, too, Gwen." He didn't stop until his body was once again flush against mine, both of his arms resting on the hedge at my back, caging me in. His smell was doing unbelievable things to my head and my insides.

I was so close to falling over the edge and he could sense it. I wanted to take the plunge, I wanted everything he could give me. I was so close to saying "yes" I couldn't breathe.

I squeezed my eyes shut and whispered, "I can't."

But he wasn't having it. "Tell me," he whispered back. My eyes snapped open again to find his searching mine, boring into them so deep I was sure he could see all of my secrets, feel every emotion. "*Please.*"

That damn *please*. It was going to get me every time. Hell, it was going to be my downfall. I became the world's biggest pushover whenever he said it. But he looked so vulnerable, like he was in agony, and I couldn't stand to see him like that if I could fix it.

So, the dam broke.

I decided to throw caution to the wind while subsequently losing my mind all in the same moment.

And damn the consequences.

I exhaled heavily, not even realizing I'd been holding my breath. "Yes," I exhaled, "I feel it, too. All the time. I can't get you out of my head. I want this, *you*, so much you—" His lips crashed down onto mine before I could finish what I was saying.

I couldn't stop the moan that released as soon as I felt his soft, full lips covering mine. He pressed his entire body against mine, pulling me in tightly like he never wanted to let go. One arm rose, his hand firmly cupping the back of my head. His other arm wrapped around my waist, his fingers spreading out and brushing the underside of my breast. His lips were hungry on mine, tasting every inch of my mouth, greedy for more like it would be his only chance to taste me. And I gave it right back, throwing myself into the kiss and wrapping my arms around his neck, pulling him even closer. All rational thoughts raced from my mind, going from zero to sixty in about half a second.

His lips tasted so much better than I'd imagined they would. I sucked hard on his tongue, drawing a deep groan from him and a shift in the angle of his head, deepening the kiss. The arm around my waist moved lower to cup my ass for a second before it started to knead my cheek. My fingers dove into his hair, pulling the strands harder as he gripped my back side, eliciting an even louder groan from him. I could feel the hard length of him against my stomach getting harder by the second, and all I wanted was for him to release it, rip my panties off, and take me right there. I had never been this ravenous with any man before.

Our moans and heavy breathing were the only sounds filling the small space and Clay suddenly tore his mouth away from mine to look deep into my eyes with so much need, I thought my legs were going to buckle. "You have no idea how long I've wanted this," he muttered as his mouth went to my neck, leaving a trail of sensual kisses and licks. "Oh, God. How long I've *needed* this."

My eyes rolled back in my head at the feel of his unbelievable mouth on the most sensitive area of my neck. His words were like a sensual caress, traveling the entire length of my body, stroking every inch and igniting warm sensations everywhere they touched. I had never been this wet in my life and the ache in that area was growing to an unbearable level the more he touched me.

"*Oh my God,* me too. This feels so good," I panted as the hand at my head moved to my breast, squeezing and massaging it through my dress. When he took my nipple between his thumb and forefinger and pinched, my toes curled and my fingers started to claw at his back, looking for purchase to keep me steady so I didn't collapse from pleasure.

"*Clay,*" I moaned, "I need to feel you." I couldn't stand it anymore. I needed his jacket off so I grabbed the lapel and ripped it off, Clay removing his hands briefly to let the material slide off his arms. His breathing was just as ragged and desperate as mine as he undid the clasp of my dress at the nape of my neck and tugged it down, revealing my lavender lace strapless bra, my breasts spilling out the top.

I had always had a small obsession with nice lingerie. Some women had a thing for shoes or purses and I had one for lace and satin undergarments in all the colors of the rainbow. In a life in which I often felt used, degraded, and unappreciated, pretty underwear made me feel confident and sexy, like a goddess. William, of course, had always approved of the obsession and preferred that I wore nothing but the nice lingerie, so he could have something to look at while he took what he wanted from me. But I didn't wear them for him. I wore them for myself.

I could definitely tell that Clay was appreciating my affinity with the garments as his eyes took in my chest. I always matched my bra and underwear to my outfits, which was more of an OCD thing than it was a vanity issue. And the way Clay was looking at my body now, with so much untamed desire, I was mentally applauding myself for my efforts. He was making me feel like the most beautiful woman in the world as his eyes raked over me.

"Jesus, you're gorgeous. So damn gorgeous." Both of this hands went to cup my breasts as he leaned in to take my mouth in another ferocious kiss. I'd always been fortunate enough to have perky C cups most of my life, and Beatrice had told me on more than one occasion that I had "a nice rack." I was definitely thankful for it now.

I had no idea, though, that I would get so much pleasure by having someone handle them the way Clay was. William had never bothered with pleasuring me and this felt *amazing*, probably even more so because it was Clay that was doing it. His lips left mine again as he stared down at his hands on my breasts.

"These are fucking perfect." His voice was low and gravelly, almost like he was angry, but I knew better. He was as turned on I was.

He yanked one cup down, exposing my bare breast to him, and leaned down to take my puckered nipple deep into his mouth. And he sucked. Hard.

It was *heaven*.

I let out a long moan and immediately latched onto his head, holding him at my chest. His tongue swirled around my nipple, his hand continuing to knead the other. "Oh God...yes. Y*esss*."

Clay moaned around my breast as I thrust my chest out, pushing further into his mouth. His mouth left me as he yanked down the other cup and went to work on my other breast. "Mmm, you taste so good. Every inch of you. I knew you would," he mumbled, his hot breath covering my nipple, making me shiver even more with want.

His words were turning me on even more, if that was possible, and I wanted to hear more. I wanted to feel more, too. My fingers flew to his shirt and grappled with the buttons. I wanted, needed, to feel his skin. If this was the only time we would be close like this, I had to feel his bare, muscled chest or I would hate myself forever.

His mouth left my breast and flew up to give me another insanely delicious kiss. As soon as I got his shirt open, I pushed him back enough so I could look my fill. His torso was tanned, toned, and perfect. He had light chest hair between his sculpted pecs and just above his waistline, an impeccable six-pack that I couldn't help but run my fingers over—though I would prefer it was my tongue doing the deed instead—and a distinct V framing his hips and waist.

Why was this man a politician and not a model? Or a freaking movie star? Seriously, he should be immortalized in marble. I should call *People* magazine right now and nominate him for the Sexiest Man Alive award. He'd win hands down and I was already planning to volunteer to take the pictures.

"You're amazing," I whispered, not taking my eyes off of the new image of all my future fantasies.

Clay let out an impatient growl and pulled me back into him, one hand going back to grab my ass. On instinct, I lifted one of my legs and wrapped it around his waist, opening myself up to him and giving him more access. He took full advantage.

He fisted the material of my dress and lifted it up until his hand could feel my panties that covered only half my cheeks. Clay released a frustrated groan as his fingers slipped inside the lace material and slid around to my front. I feathered kisses all over his neck, his smell almost sending me over the edge. Not to mention what his bare chest rubbing up against my nipples was doing to me. Feeling his heated skin against mine was pure magic.

Then, his fingers found my sex, and I had to bite down on his shoulder to prevent myself from screaming at the top of my lungs.

Instead, I released a long moan at the contact. No one had touched me down there in such a non-violent way in years and I thought I'd die from the incredible pleasure it shot through my body. Thoughts of the bruises on my thighs and waist—tokens of William's most recent drunken bedroom escapades—briefly flashed through my mind. I was grateful that Clay wasn't lifting my dress up any further because they were ugly and very obvious and I didn't want anything to ruin this moment with him. I cleared my head of anything negative and gave over to the divine euphoria that was Clay Masterson.

He cupped my mound and gently ran his fingers through my soft folds. "Fuck," he breathed out on a large exhale, "you are so wet for me." He started rubbing his fingers faster, applying more pressure. "It's all for me, isn't it Gwen? All of that's for me. Only me." On the last word, he plunged his finger inside me and immediately started pumping it in and out.

"Aaahhh! Yes, Clay. *Yes.*" My orgasm was so close. This did not have to go on long before I was going to lose it. In fact, I could probably lose it just from his kisses, they were so intoxicating.

"Say it. I need you to say it. This is all for me." My eyes flew open at his words. He was panting like he was on the edge too, but he was speaking in a very serious tone. His eyes were focused on mine when I met them. He looked so intense, so passionate, and he was looking at *me*. It was all for *me*. I couldn't help the sense of pride I felt when I realized I was turning a man like Clay Masterson on. *I* was making him feel like this.

When I didn't respond right away, his eyes flared, the hand on my neck tightened, and he thrust his fingers even deeper inside me. "Say it, Gwen," he demanded.

"It's all for you. Only you," I breathed. I kept my eyes locked onto his with every word I spoke. It was a heady moment as we stared at each other, so many unsaid things passing between us. I felt like something more than just lust was happening between us. I couldn't, and wouldn't, put it into words at the moment, but something clearly changed between us with those words. Our entire dynamic was shifting. At least, that's what it felt like to me and I hoped he felt the same.

As Clay's fingers continued to thrust inside me, the hand I had on his chest traveled down and cupped his arousal through his pants. His head flew back in pleasure as he closed his eyes and let out a loud moan that was music to my ears. I loved hearing the noises this man made. There was nothing sexier. I rubbed my palm along his length, my fingers grabbing onto his girth, stroking as much as I could get ahold of. Yeah, he was *huge*. I had never been with anyone his size and it conjured all sorts of images in my brain.

How would he feel inside of me? What does he like in bed, and out of bed? Oh, how I wanted to find out.

His body shuddered as I stroked his length and cupped his balls. *"Gwen..."* His head dipped forward and his fingers inside me went deeper, faster, stroking my inner walls at an almost frantic pace. "Shit, that feels good. I want you so fucking bad."

I wanted him, too. Way more than I thought was possible and way more than was good for me. I chased the ache that was building rapidly in my core, wanting nothing more than to give myself over to ecstasy. Nothing else existed but me and Clay. There was no election or charity luncheons or angry fiancés. My entire world was anchored in this moment, this exquisite pleasure that was dominating every inch of my body. I felt like I couldn't catch my breath and I started to feel my core clenching around his fingers.

Just as I was about to scream out my release, I heard voices on the path, mere feet from where we were hidden among the hedges.

We both froze. His fingers still deep inside me and mine still grasping his hardness. I was sure my eyes were as big as saucers right now and no doubt Clay could feel my hammering pulse. Hell, he could probably hear it, it was so out of control. *We're going to get caught. My life will be ruined. His career will be ruined.*

Oh, God. Please, no.

To my undeniable relief, the people were already walking down the path away from us. The whole thing hadn't lasted more than a minute, but it had been long enough for me to have a head-on collision with reality.

What. The. Hell. Am I doing?

The ache from my impending orgasm that was about to send me into a blissful pleasure coma only minutes before was long gone. My heart was still beating like a snare drum in my chest but not from lust. Now it was from panic. We could have been caught. So easily caught. By anyone!

I ripped my hand off of Clay as if he had burned me and pushed at his chest until he stumbled back a few steps, causing his fingers to pull out of me in one swift, painful motion. I reluctantly met his eyes and instead of the burning desire I saw moments ago, they were now filled with apologies and, maybe a little frustration, but mostly understanding. He looked like he wanted to say something, but he could tell the moment was over and that I was clearly freaking out. Majorly.

He sighed heavily and started to right his clothing. I frantically straightened my bra and fastened the clasp of my dress, all the while feeling like I was about to hyperventilate. I was so incredibly stupid. *How could I let myself get carried away like that?*

I could see him out of my peripheral vision adjusting himself inside his pants and buttoning up his shirt. He reached down and grabbed his jacket that had landed on the grass, slipping it back on and adjusting his tie.

I honestly had no idea what to say. I felt like I should be embarrassed but strangely, I wasn't. Everything that happened with this man just always felt so right, including this. Which was crazy! My heart was now beating like a snare drum on crack.

He stepped forward looking like he was going to reach for me but I stepped back away from him. He immediately stopped, his forehead furrowing like that action had hurt him. I didn't want to hurt him. For crying out loud, I wanted to touch him everywhere. But I knew that I wouldn't want him to let go if he got close enough again, and I really needed to get my head together.

Before my mind could formulate words, he beat me to it. "Look, I'm not going to apologize for what just happened. I'm sure I should but I can't because I don't regret it and to be honest, I'd do it again. I *want* to do it again, Gwen." He gave me a pointed look and blocked my path to the archway that led out to path. To my escape.

"We can't, Clay. I can't even believe I did that. We shouldn't have and I'm sorry that I allowed it to happen." I kept my eyes downcast because I didn't want to see hurt in his eyes again.

He let out a frustrated huff and said, "Don't do this. You wanted that just as much as I did. Everything we said was the truth and you know it." His voice turned softer, almost pleading. "Please. Don't go backwards. What just happened was amazing. Don't deny what's between us."

Oh God, I didn't want to but what else could I do? How was this supposed to work without us getting caught? I bit down on my lip to stop the tears that were threatening to spill over. "Please let me go. I can't think straight right now. I just need some time alone." My voice was barely a whisper.

When he stayed silent, I hesitantly looked up. His expression looked thoughtful, like he was contemplating something—I was sure I didn't want to know what—but he didn't argue further. "Fine, but you listen to me." His demanding tone gave me no choice but to pay attention. "This isn't over. This, and more, will happen again. I *will* have you, Gwen. And this," he said, motioning between us, "only made me want you more. I can't give up now and I won't." He bent forward slightly to bring his face right in front of mine. "I don't care about your fiancé, I don't care about the election, I don't care about whatever excuses you're going to come up with for why this shouldn't happen. You *will* be mine, Gwen. I promise you."

With that, he walked away, leaving me standing there with a heavy heart and a lump in my throat. Two seconds after he left my eyesight, my brain kicked into overdrive.

What the hell does that mean? I'm going to be *his*?

How was I supposed to react to that? Whatever was going through his head, he'd been completely serious, that much I could tell.

He meant whatever he'd said.

I just wished that I understood it.

I started to get a sinking feeling in my stomach when I realized that what we did just now, what just happened, had changed everything.

Oh, crap. What have I done?

CHAPTER NINE

APOLOGIES AND AVOIDANCE

Clay

A few days later, I still couldn't get Gwen and that afternoon in the garden out of my head. I'd been thinking about her nonstop since I left her standing there with her hair mussed and her cheeks flushed. The woman was consuming me. I've *never* reacted to a woman that way in my entire life. I practically attacked her, for Christ's sake.

Before that afternoon I had decided not to pursue anything with this woman. It was way too risky and the potential exposure would destroy both of us. I mean, the citizens of Washington, D.C. don't want the man who could potentially be their mayor to have an affair with an engaged woman. I'd be labeled as a philanderer and my career would probably never recover. And it would be worse for Gwen. Who knows what the media would call her, and the Callahan family would undoubtedly ensure that she took all the blame in order to protect their reputation. What I had done was so incredibly reckless.

But *damn*, she had been so responsive.

Her body had come alive under my hands, and while I knew there was fire underneath that façade of the prim and proper lady she had adopted, I still hadn't expected that intense of a response. She had been all heat and passion and gave back as good as she got. She had been the hottest thing that I'd ever held in my arms, no question. Her body was firm and tight but soft in all the right places and my reaction to her was the evidence. I had almost taken her right there, against the bushes, at a public event, where anyone could have seen us. I had been completely ruled by my urges alone and had given absolutely no thought to the consequences.

That *never* happened to me.

Nobody affected me to the point where I threw control and common sense out the window. But this woman, this amazingly sexy, intelligent, funny woman was turning everything upside down.

And she belongs to someone else.

That acknowledgment was like a douse of cold water on the arousal that was now tenting my pants, all caused by thoughts of Gwen. All I ever had to do was just think about her and I was gone. Regardless though, I had to remember that she was William Callahan's fiancé and as much of a prick as that man might be, it wasn't any of my business. And it was his ring she wore on her finger.

But I can't help but involve myself, dammit. Every time I told myself to just forget about her, she crawled her way back inside my head. And every instinct inside me said that I was supposed to be near this woman, that somehow she was meant to be in my life.

That had also never happened to me. I'd never had feelings this strong for anyone and I certainly had never considered a long-term future with any woman I'd been involved with in the past. It wasn't the right time in my life to get serious with anyone.

I knew all of this and it didn't matter how many times I said it. I still wanted her.

I was so fucked.

For the rest of the day, I made it a point to keep myself busy and distracted with work. I had meetings with David and the rest of my advisors about the upcoming events I would be attending, as well as developing our platforms for the debates and campaign rallies next month. I had to be on my game if I was going to be any kind of threat to William Callahan. The man was ruthless but I knew I'd be a better advocate for the people of D.C. I just had to make sure the people knew that.

This was what I always did if there was something going on in my life that I couldn't escape from or wasn't sure how to handle. I threw myself into work. And it worked beautifully, until David unknowingly shoved the one woman I didn't want to think about back into the forefront of my mind. *That asshole.*

"Callahan's fiancé does a lot of charity and volunteer work, which definitely looks good for him and makes him look more like 'the people's candidate.'" He sat across from me in the leather chair in front of my desk, pouring over schedules and data. "I wouldn't be surprised if he forces her into all of that," he murmured with a note of disgust in his voice. David had told me recently that it wasn't exactly a secret in D.C. society that Callahan seemed a little too controlling of Gwen, and apparently, it was one more reason for David to dislike the man. He'd never exactly held him in high esteem.

Well, neither did I.

The words flew out of my mouth before I even stopped to think about what I was saying. "No, that's all her. She actually cares about helping people. That bastard has nothing to do with it," I snapped.

I couldn't disguise the pure malice that dripped from my words even if I tried. I hated thinking about her with that man, and the fact that I was running against him only intensified my contempt towards him.

David abruptly stopped shuffling through papers at the harshness of my tone and looked up at me through his black frame glasses with a raised eyebrow, waiting for me to elaborate. I didn't want to give any kind of explanation, so he got impatient and asked for one.

"You've hardly said a word for the past twenty minutes and then that comes out of your mouth out of nowhere. Is there something you'd like to share with the class?"

I shrugged casually and said in a noncommittal tone, "I just don't like the man. He's a privileged, egotistical prick, but his fiancé actually seems like a sweet person. I have no idea how he was able to hook a woman like that but he doesn't deserve her, that's for sure." *Shit.* I immediately knew that I'd said too much.

David narrowed his eyes at me, looking suspicious. "You seem to have a pretty strong opinion about this. Do you know her or something?"

Avoiding his gaze but keeping my voice calm, I answered, "No, I've just met her a couple of times. We didn't talk long but it's obvious she's nothing like him." I hoped that was enough to quash any suspicion he had about why I had a strong opinion about another man's betrothed.

He stared at me for another moment before he spoke. "Well, she doesn't talk to the press much, so I don't know much about her aside from what's public knowledge so I'll take your word for it. Let's go over topics for Friday's meeting."

With that, his attention went back to the files in his lap and mine went to the woman who was taking up permanent residence in my head. David left twenty minutes later and I was left alone again in my office.

Alone with my thoughts.

Thoughts that were primarily centered on one woman.

Great.

Realizing I wasn't going to get any more work done with Gwen on the brain, I gave up and did something I probably shouldn't have. In fact, I *knew* I shouldn't have but in that moment, I only had one thing on my mind. Only one thing was going to satisfy me. It was desperate and it was crazy but I needed to talk to her.

I pulled out my phone and scrolled down to the name I added into my contacts earlier that afternoon. I knew how wrong it was to use my resources to get her number but again, I didn't give a shit. I was like a man possessed and Gwen McKindry had all of the control.

I did the most dangerous thing I could have done.

And I silently prayed that this wouldn't come back to bite me in the ass.

Gwen

I rode in the back of the town car, feeling like I always did when I left the homeless shelter: powerless. I tried to help those on the streets in any way that I could by bringing clothing, food, and even helping some of the adults find jobs. I helped in the daycare when I could, served in the soup kitchen when needed, and donated funds to the shelters around the city that were most in need. It broke my heart to hear the stories of these people. Most of them just got dealt a bad hand in life and had no one to help them get on their feet.

Sometimes, all it takes is one person to help turn someone's life around. One helping hand could be all that's needed to make a difference.

And I felt like I could be that person for so many of them, I wanted to be that person for them. But for all the money and notoriety I had, I had very little power. And it made me feel guilty as hell. William may approve of me helping at the shelters and doing various volunteer work, but he positively abhorred doing it himself. He did occasionally whenever he needed new pictures of him working hand-in-hand with the people, but he would never actually do it out of the goodness of his heart. I'm pretty sure he thought that he was going to get a disease by even stepping foot into an impoverished area. The newspapers should re-word their headlines to read "Man of the Middle and Upper-class People Only" because he could care less about the poor.

I was so distracted by my troubled thoughts that I almost didn't hear my phone beep with a text. The only people that ever texted me were Beatrice or Felicity, so I assumed that it had to be one of them. William always called if he had to talk to me and my parents only ever contacted me whenever they needed me to do something, like give an interview or make an appearance somewhere. All for the sake of the McKindry name, of course.

I pulled my phone out of my purse and saw a number I didn't recognize pop up on the screen. I didn't give my cell phone number out to anybody because the last thing I needed was reporters getting ahold of it and calling me at all hours of the day and night. Confused, I unlocked it and opened up the message. I read it and my stomach did a flip.

Unknown number: *Hey, it's Clay. I'm sorry for contacting you. I know I shouldn't and I don't want to make you uncomfortable. I just wanted to see how you were.*

It was *him*.

Clay.

Wait, what?

How in the hell did he get my number?

Me: *How did you get my number?*

His response came almost immediately.

Clay: *I have my ways. How are you?*

How was I supposed to handle this? I mean, sure, we made out in the garden once, but I had no intention whatsoever of allowing that to happen again—despite the fact that I was aching for him like a lovesick teenager—and resuming contact of any type between each other had disaster written all over it. I should just delete his messages and not even reply again. That was the best way to avoid a catastrophe of astronomical proportions.

But, of course, curiosity got the better of me. Or stupidity. I'm not really sure which.

Me: *We shouldn't be talking.*

Why had he contacted me in the first place? Had he been thinking about me and that afternoon, too? Surely not. He could have any woman he wanted and we had just been caught up in the moment, nothing more.

So why did I feel like it had been more? Why did I *want* it to be more?

Clay: *I know and I'm sorry but I just needed to apologize.*

My heart fell. Apologize?

Me: *For what?*

Clay: *For my behavior the other day. I should never have put you in that position and I hope you can forgive me. It won't happen again.*

All traces of excitement and hopefulness instantly fled as I read his words. He was apologizing for *that*? He regretted it? Was he just sorry because I had a fiancé and it was wrong or because he regretted doing it with me specifically? And if the second, what does that say about *me*?

And it was never going to happen again? That was the worst part to read, if I was being honest with myself. The sense of disappointment I felt at reading that was much stronger than basic rationale could explain.

Wait, what am I saying? I should be happy that this won't happen again because it shouldn't have happened in the first place. He's the only one who's making any sense here. I had to tell myself to put aside whatever feelings I'd developed for this man. We had crossed a boundary that afternoon and we could not, absolutely not, cross it again.

Me: *No need to apologize. I was as much at fault as you. But you're right, it won't happen again.*

His response this time didn't come as quickly as the others.

Clay: *Right. So, we're okay?*

No, because I don't know where this leaves us.

Gah, there is no us! Get that through your head, Gwen!

Me: *Of course. Already forgotten.*

Not even close.

Clay: *Great. I'm sure I'll see you around then.*

Me: *Most likely.*

I turned my phone on silent after that last text. I didn't want to talk to anyone for a few minutes. He said everything that needed to be said and yet, I was left feeling bereft, like the state of euphoria that I'd been living in since the luncheon had been suddenly obliterated, leaving my stupid heart scarred. I couldn't believe that I'd actually let that man in, that I'd been foolish enough to open myself up to him.

What the hell is wrong with me? I wasn't this person. I didn't get swept away in fairy tales where my knight in shining armor came to rescue me and we rode off into the sunset, living happily ever after. There was a reason I didn't write fantasy or romance novels: I just didn't believe them. That wasn't real life.

I needed to forget Clay Masterson before I risked losing more than just my heart.

I sat at the dining room table staring down at the delicious-looking beef wellington—our housekeeper, Pam, was also our cook and one of the best in the entire city—with both longing and disgust. Longing because I wanted to eat it so bad but disgust because my stomach was apparently not as hungry as my head thought that it was.

I blamed my conflicted appetite on one man. No, it wasn't the deplorable man sitting across from me at the other end of the table, tapping away at his iPad, though it usually was and for obvious reasons. No, this game of I'm-hungry-but-I-can't-bring-myself-to-shove-this-food-down-my-throat was all because of a charming, irresistible, tall, dark and handsome politician. *Clay Masterson.*

Clay. Freaking. Masterson.

It had been two days since he texted me, but my mind kept going through everything that he'd said in the garden that day and then everything he'd said in his texts. In the garden, he had said everything with such assuredness, like there was no doubt that he would make all of what he said happen. But then in his texts, it was like he'd completely changed his mind about the entire situation. Had he even meant what he said that day or had he just been swept up in the passion of the moment? There was no real way of knowing at this point.

In the two days since we'd last talked, I'd tried to write a few chapters of my book, but I couldn't concentrate on anything beyond what had happened among those hedges. Note to self: consider "among the hedges" for possible book title. The only things I felt compelled to write were love scenes and intimate, heated moments between my characters and it sickened me. Every time I pictured the male lead in my head, an image of Clay would appear instead. Every time there was an intense scene between the characters, somehow they would always end up on the bed in a tangled frenzy.

It was like I couldn't escape this man even in the fictional world. One would think that I'd never even been touched by a man before Clay with the way I was acting. But, with him, it had kind of felt that way. No man had ever touched me the way he had, and it felt like I was experiencing my own sensuality for the first time. And he'd brought that out of me. With his heated kisses and magical fingers, he made me feel like a woman, a real woman, who was wanted by a man in the most carnal sense. That didn't sound like the most romantic notion, but deep down, everyone longed to be desired on a physical level—it was human nature. That yearning for a deep, physical connection with another person was embedded in our psyches and was part of our basic physiology.

Though some part of me knew all these things, until Clay, I hadn't fully realized what I'd been missing. Now, I understood on a very intimate level how intoxicating having that connection with someone can be. Finally feeling that unbridled passion for someone and allowing those primal urges to take over had completely altered my entire reality. It opened up new doors for me, allowed me to see other possibilities.

Now, it felt like I was walking through life at a normal pace, but I was walking through it backwards. So I everything I saw, I saw from a new prospective and I had no idea where I was going next. It was exciting because everything felt brand new, but it was also scary as hell because there was no way of knowing what to expect.

And although the physical chemistry between us was explosive and the desire insatiable, for me at least, this attraction went deeper than simple lust. I was drawn to Clay as an individual. He was smart and witty, funny, caring, and genuine. I could actually see myself falling for a man like him, and I had the sneaky suspicion that my heart was already headed down that road.

Though I knew we could never have a future together, I couldn't help the overwhelming feelings of loss and sadness that came over me whenever I remembered what he'd said in the garden and why I couldn't be with Clay. Before I met him, it had been easier to resign myself to this life and accept that I would never experience the type of love I longed for with the type of man who would cherish me for the rest of our lives together. I had been ignorant of the possibility of having such a connection with someone, of feeling that pull towards another human being. It wasn't that I didn't believe in love, but I had just never encountered an emotion so strong, nor encountered a man who evoked such powerful feelings from me.

That all changed with Clay and it had become so much worse to endure since he'd given me a taste of what it could be like with him. I felt like my feelings had tripled since our tryst in the garden. And even though it had probably been the most spectacular experience of my life, I almost wished that it had never happened. Since I knew it could never happen again, nor go any further than we had already allowed it to, I was better off not even knowing what it was supposed to be like with a real man.

And the second my thoughts strayed to my fiancé, all notions of surrendering to an amorous, clandestine affair with the most potent man I'd ever met, came to a screeching halt and I floated down from my cloud and back to earth.

Excitement and desire were soon replaced with fear and caution when I considered the consequences of such a thing. I berated myself for thinking that such a relationship was even possible while I was engaged to William. He had eyes all over the city and there was absolutely no way I could hide something so scandalous.

My body literally shivered at the thought of what he would do to me and Clay if we did engage in such a thing and were discovered. I knew beyond a doubt that he would strike at both of us with untamed wrath and ruthless determination to teach us both a lesson. I knew if he was pushed that far, to the point where fury overtook him and he simply couldn't control his actions, nothing and no one would stop him. Even the possibility of losing the election, if not his entire career.

I couldn't allow that to happen. I had experienced William's anger before so I knew what to expect from him but Clay didn't. He had no idea how far my fiancé would go to enact revenge if he felt threatened in any way. I just couldn't bear to think of William hurting Clay and I refused to endanger him, to expose him to William's madness.

Which was all fine, anyway, because Clay basically said that he had no interest in doing so and that our one heated, passionate moment would never be repeated. I was just making myself feel better by justifying that decision as I mulled over everything that could happen if people found out. Those dark thoughts eased my anxiety somewhat. I tried to convince myself that I was agreeing to keep our distance from each other in order to protect both of us. That sounded much better than the truth. That I was actually pining for him, and he probably regretted ever getting involved with me in the first place.

At least this way, I didn't feel quite as pathetic.

I shook my head, clearing it, and focused all of my attention on the asparagus on my untouched plate.

"How was your day?" William asked, startling me from my thoughts and causing my head to snap up in his direction.

"Good," I replied, forcing a smile. If I didn't want him to suspect that anything out of the ordinary had been going on, I couldn't respond any differently than I normally would to his questions. "I think I've decided on a design for the invitations, so that's a relief."

He just nodded and kept his head down, his attention still focused on his tablet, which I was grateful for because it meant I didn't have to look into his eyes. I wanted to make sure to keep him happy and calm this evening and to give him no excuse to snap at me. Not that it usually took anything more than an eyebrow raise to piss him off but that was typically if alcohol was involved.

He usually liked hearing about the wedding plans. Not because he actually cared about the details, but the fact that we were getting closer to being legally bound together seemed to have a calming effect on him. It was almost like he needed the reassurance that it was still happening.

"Next Saturday we're going to go to the Nationals game, so I'll need you to clear your schedule that day," he muttered, his focus still on the tablet. "Apparently, it's some kind of Campaign Day or something. Several politicians will be there, so they're going to do some press stuff before the game, and Rachel set it up to where I'm going to throw out the first pitch. Said the family atmosphere will be good for my image and will help in the polls."

"That's great. It'll be a fun afternoon."

Even though I would have to endure the day with him, I was excited. I loved baseball and hadn't been to a game in ages. William didn't care for the sport and he was never willing to attend a game with me. Nevertheless, it would probably be a nice break from all of the wedding planning and the monotony of the social scene that I had to endure even more of lately because of the fast-approaching election.

William gave a sarcastic snort and said, "Well, it better help in the polls if I'm going to sit there for three damn hours."

I ignored that comment and continued to push the food around on my plate.

"I have to go to New York the weekend after that, too," he said through a mouth full of food.

That was news to me. "Oh? What for?" I asked, hoping that I wasn't expected to go.

"I'm meeting with the mayor. If I can get his endorsement for the campaign, Masterson won't stand a chance. Not that he has one either way, but I'm going to make sure he doesn't even have a prayer of coming close."

He chuckled to himself, a maniacal chuckle that only he could make sound eerie, and continued to shove food into his mouth.

I honestly didn't care where he went or why, but I was already looking forward to an entire weekend home alone. Maybe I could invite Beatrice and Felicity over and we could have a girl's night. The good indoors kind with movies, pizza and *lots* of wine. We hadn't had one of those in so long and I could really use it. William, of course, never liked them coming over if he was home. He liked my friends about as much as they liked him, which is to say not at all.

"So, you'll be gone all weekend?" I asked, hopefully but hesitantly. I couldn't sound too excited.

His eyes snapped up to mine and narrowed with a questioning look. *Oh, crap. Here we go.*

"Why? What are you planning to do while I'm gone?" His voice was hard but his tone was even. He wasn't angry…yet.

I shrugged casually, acting like it didn't matter to me either way how long he was gone. "I'll probably just get some wedding planning done. I just wanted to know in case I had to book appointments. I wouldn't want to be busy the whole weekend if you plan to be back early." The lie fell so easily from my lips as I waited for his reaction.

He hesitated a moment but then the crease in his forehead smoothed and he nodded his head slightly, seeming satisfied with my answer.

"That's fine. I should be gone most of the day Saturday and won't be back until late Sunday night. My flight doesn't leave until early Saturday evening, but I'll be working at the office most of that day."

"Alright," I said, trying my best to hide the state of glee I was now in.

With everything going on lately, I was missing my friends more than usual, and thanks to my recent escapades with a certain blue-eyed Adonis, I could really use some girl time.

And probably some of that wine.

CHAPTER TEN

HEARTS AND DIAMONDS

Gwen

June

Saturday was the day of the Nationals game and I woke up in an exceptionally good mood. The sun was streaming through the bedroom windows when I woke up and William had already left to do some work at the office, so I had the entire morning to drink my coffee on the back patio in peace. The weather was beautiful for a baseball game and I just had a feeling that I would enjoy myself, no matter how hard William tried to ruin it.

The game started at 12:20 in the afternoon and William and I had to be at Nationals Park by 11:00 for the pre-game press events. Since my internal clock would rarely let me sleep past 7:30, I had plenty of time to lounge on the patio, go for a refreshing swim in the pool, and take a luxuriously long, hot shower. I looked at myself in the mirror after my shower and saw what could have almost passed as a new person. My skin was a little sun-kissed and still slightly pink from the hot water, the ever-present bags under my eyes were all but invisible thanks to eight, uninterrupted hours of sleep the previous night, and my eyes looked a brighter blue than normal.

I looked healthy. If anyone who didn't know me well had seen me then, I'd probably look, dare I say it, *happy*. And maybe I was. Not necessarily with my life in general, but I could admit that my particularly positive disposition that morning was probably due to the dreams I had last night about a certain horrifically handsome politician. *Oh yes*, I had dreams about Clay and they had woken me up up with a smile on my face and a wetness between my legs. Who could be in a bad mood after that?

Sure, I knew I shouldn't be thinking about him, but I had also come to the decision that I wasn't going to let anything more happen between us, so I saw no harm in remembering our one amazingly hot, closer-to-fantasy-than-real-life moment. It was all in my head now so there was no danger whatsoever. I figured it would hit me later that I may never experience that kind of passion again for the rest of my life and I would get terribly depressed over it. But just for today, for just a little while, I was going to be content with the little bit that I had.

Though, to my complete surprise and bewilderment, he texted me again yesterday. I had to read it almost twenty times before I was going to believe what I was seeing.

The text had said, "I can't stop thinking about you."

And I still hadn't responded.

I couldn't believe he'd actually admitted that. I would have sooner sawed every one of my fingers off before I would have confessed to him that he was all I thought about. After the disbelief wore off, I allowed myself to be unabashedly pleased with the fact that I, Gwen McKindry, was occupying the thoughts of Clay Masterson. And I didn't want to ruin it by responding and giving him the opportunity to take it back. So, I selfishly pocketed that text, allowing the words to float through my head for the rest of the day and throughout the night.

I was in such a state of bliss that I had also called Felicity and planned for a girl's night at my house next Saturday night, to which she squeaked out a "hell yes!" and maybe a few "yee haws" somewhere in there. I couldn't exactly tell because her squawking usually ran together into one long high-pitched squeal.

So, I had some time with my girls coming, the man I was shamelessly crushing on couldn't stop thinking about me, and the sun was shining.

For a brief moment in time, everything in my world felt *right*.

I got dressed in my white Nationals jersey because they were playing at home, a red t-shirt underneath, denim shorts, and my favorite red Keds. Even though I would probably sweat like a pig, I was not allowed to *look* like I was sweating like a pig, so I wore my hair down in loose curls. My mother always told me that I had to look cool, calm, and perfect, no matter how ridiculously uncomfortable you were. Hopefully, I wouldn't sweat off all of my makeup until after the press stuff. We would be in a private box during the actual game so that would help.

William arrived at the house at 10:30, came inside to pick up a few things and make sure I was ready, and then led me back outside to the car where Roberto was waiting patiently to drive us to the field.

"Won't you be hot in your suit?" I asked William, noting he still wore the jacket and tie he wore to the office. Not that I actually cared whether he was burning up or not because I sure as hell didn't.

"Rachel will have a jersey for me that I'll put on before I get in front of the cameras." He fiddled with his BlackBerry and barely looked up at me as he spoke. Though he rushed me out of the house and into the car, I didn't miss the scent of whiskey on him. *Geez, it wasn't even noon yet.* And he would no doubt have more than a couple beers at the game. I was already having to force myself to stay relaxed and not let my anxiety get the better of me.

We arrived at Nationals Park with ten minutes to spare but were immediately ushered to the press area as soon as we stepped out of the car. Rachel rushed over and started going over lines and comments for the cameras with both of us. They probably wouldn't address me but Rachel always wanted us prepared.

Some idiot reporter from a gossip magazine could always be there and throw us a curve ball, pun intended, and ask me if we were planning on having children anytime soon, or something personal like that. It had happened before and had been about as awkward as one might imagine. The last time I got asked that exact question was by some callous vulture at a breast cancer awareness banquet because yes, I just loved to discuss the joys of having children around women who had either survived having a debilitating disease or who were still fighting for their lives. I had sure set that reporter straight.

The press events were taking place under a large tent in an area just inside the front gates. As soon as we entered the tent, William was swept away by Rachel and a few of his other colleagues that I recognized, while I made my way over to the refreshments table for a glass of lemonade that looked heavenly in this humidity. I didn't have much to do until the cameras officially turned on, at which time I'd be forced to stand behind William with a pleasant smile and play the role of supportive, loyal fiancé. Definitely wasn't looking forward to that, but the fresh lemonade I was currently gulping down was certainly helping.

"I do hope you've saved some lemonade for the rest of us," came a deep, male voice from somewhere behind me, startling me. The voice was close enough that I could feel his breath at my ear, and I wondered how I didn't notice his presence. I stepped forward slightly and whipped around, knowing full well who I was going to see. After all it was *his* voice that taunted me day and night. I had memorized it without even trying to and, whether or not I wanted to, would recognize it anywhere.

I turned around and came face-to-face with the very man who had invaded my dreams and had the ability to turn my insides into liquid, scrambling my brain processes into neuron mayhem every time I was around him.

Of course, he would be here. Even though this was Campaign Day, I never once considered the fact that Clay would be here. He'd told me that day in his office that he had played baseball in college, so of course he would have been invited to attend. How could I have been so clueless? I was definitely not prepared to see him today, especially with William standing ten feet away. I had ignored that last text, hoping it would discourage him from contacting me again. Apparently, he didn't get the message or he simply didn't care.

"Clay," I said, so low it was barely audible. I was so surprised with his presence I couldn't manage anything louder than a whisper. "Wh-what are you doing here?"

The way he looked at me told me he was thinking back to the afternoon in the garden. And he wore a cocky smirk on his face, as if he knew exactly what he did to me and was quite proud of himself for it. I couldn't help but remember that same moment we had together and heat instantly enveloped my entire body at the memory. I wanted to scream at my body for the reaction. I told myself that I could not get involved with this man, which meant that I had to stop looking at him through lust-clouded lenses.

"I'm throwing out the first pitch, well one of them. I'm told I'll technically be throwing the second one. After your fiancé, I believe." He acted so cool and calm, as though he were talking with any one of his associates rather than with the woman whose body he had ravaged in the garden only days before. "And one of my good friends plays for the Red Sox so I had tickets to the game regardless."

His demeanor had shifted so dramatically that I became confused. Perhaps I read him wrong and that sort of thing was so commonplace for him he barely gave the brief dalliance an afterthought at all. Had I really been so naïve to believe his confessions of having feelings for me? He'd sounded so sincere but I suppose, with enough practice, he could make any woman swoon at those words.

I suddenly felt very humiliated and foolish at my teenage impulses and imbecilic romantic notions. I learned the harsh lesson early on in life that everybody had an angle they were always working. And usually the thing that separated one person from another was the means by which they worked said angle. Apparently, all it took for me to forget that were a pair of blue eyes and broad shoulders.

Shaking myself out of my mental scolding, I replied, "Of course. Well, it was good to see you." I should probably get away from him as fast as I could before anyone realized that we were more than mere acquaintances.

His brow furrowed at my curt response. "Did I say something wrong? It's obvious I've upset you somehow, and if you'll tell me how to fix it, I'll be happy to do so immediately," he said in a low voice so only I could hear him.

Although I was turned to leave and knew that I should, something in his voice forced me to turn back around. I could see the cocky smirk was gone and had been replaced by a look of concern and was that…hurt? I couldn't be sure if that's what I saw flash in his eyes, but he definitely looked more vulnerable than I had ever seen him and my heart melted.

My God, I'm easy with this man.

"No, you haven't." I looked around to ensure no one was close enough to overhear and lowered my voice further. "I've already told you that nothing can happen. It's best if we don't speak to each other anymore."

"You don't want that. I know you don't." His voice was no longer gentle but more forceful, demanding. He almost sounded angry. "You can't deny what happened in the garden, Gwen. You cannot stand here and say that it didn't mean something to you because I damn well know that it did."

Yeah, he was angry. Well, that only served to rile me up because I had a right to be angry, too. I hadn't planned this, nor did I want it. True, I may want *him* but I didn't want the stress of this situation.

"It was just a kiss. That was all it was and all it will ever be. A weak moment on both of our parts and now we can forget about it and move on with our lives. The end."

His eyes flashed at my words and he took a step closer to me, which caused me to take a step back. I didn't need us to look like we were sharing a very intimate conversation. "If you think I'm going to forget what happened, or let you forget it for that matter, then you don't know me that well," he said roughly.

"I don't know you at all and you don't know me." I looked back toward the press stage for William and spotted him off to the side with his back turned to me while he spoke to a few other men in suits. "We can't have this conversation here. Please, Clay, just let this go," I pleaded. I needed him to let it go so I could get back to my normal life, as bleak as that sounded.

"I can't, Gwen. I've already told you that. And you'll realize that you can't either. It may take you some time to figure out that there's something here between us, something that's not just going to go away, but you will. And when you do, I'll be waiting. Until then, I'm not going to give up."

I was so stunned by that brazen proclamation that I had no idea what to say. I had never met a man who was so brash, who was so confident in his pursuits and who said precisely what was on his mind. It was confusing and made my head spin.

Before I could form a response, he lightly touched my elbow and, with a pointed look that said much more than we could say aloud in front of members of the press and my fiancé, he walked away in the direction of the small stage.

I snapped out of my Clay fog when the condensation on my glass of lemonade, that I forgot I was even holding, started to drip down my leg. I knocked back the last of it in three quick gulps, not caring about how unladylike the act was, and wished the drink had contained some level of alcohol because I could have sure used a drink.

The pre-game press interviews had gone off without a hitch. William was ever the charmer, flashing his toothy smile to the cameras and regaling the reporters with baseball father-son bonding tales, which were about as real as Rachel's augmented breasts. Somehow, his exaggerated anecdotes and All-American boy charisma were enough to mask his pompous personality. I could easily see through the ruse but I seemed to be the only one.

What was surprising was how riveting Clay's interview had been. The press, of course, asked about his career as one of the best college pitchers of his era, but he responded to those questions with disinterested comments, seeming almost embarrassed by the praise.

What captured my interest, and much of the audience's it seemed, were his stories of how he grew up playing baseball with his best friend, Parker Cruz, who now played third base for the Boston Red Sox. Clay's entire demeanor had changed when he spoke of how he'd met his friend as a kid when he was playing baseball in a park one day and how they were later able to play on the same high school and college teams. His face and voice became animated as he told his stories, making the entire audience laugh in appreciation. Although he was certainly a charmer and had a talent for public speaking, he was sincerely humble about his baseball career. He clearly loved the game but accepted when his career had come to an end, and he obviously had a genuine friendship with his best friend that made him even more endearing.

I knew next to nothing about how he grew up, let alone his friendship with a professional baseball player, and I found myself becoming enraptured in his stories, dying to know more about him. The more I learned about the man, the more I liked him. It was becoming harder and harder to find something, anything, wrong with him. Sure, he had small faults like being a little overbearing and a bit cocky, but I found that I surprisingly didn't mind those qualities in him. No, I needed something that would completely turn me off, something repulsive that would erase any feelings of affection for him.

But no such luck, yet. There had to be something, though. I mean, *my God*, the man couldn't be perfect.

These thoughts consumed my mind as we made our way down to the field, while I watched William work the cameras once again as he stood near home plate with his Nationals jersey on over his shirt and tie. I thought he looked so out of place with the jersey on, it was almost laughable. He hated this sport and yet here he was, acting like he spent his most memorable childhood years with skinned up knees and a ball in his hands.

Yeah, right.

Clay, on the other hand. Well, he looked like he belonged on a field. He had taken his jacket and tie off, unbuttoned the top few buttons at his neck and rolled up his sleeves to his forearms. Instead of a jersey, he just had a Washington Nationals baseball cap on, but he wore it well. *Very well*. Not all men could pull off baseball caps but Clay did and my mouth practically watered at the sight.

He was also standing on the field near home plate talking to reporters, along with other politicians who were able to attend. A gentleman with a comb over and a microphone spoke as his voice boomed over the PA system, drawing the crowd's attention to home plate. It was fifteen minutes until game time so people were still finding their seats, but there were enough in the stands to have an audience.

The announcer introduced all of the guests of Campaign Day, meaning all of the politicians who will be running in the upcoming elections and would like you to remember their names on the ballot sheet come November. I stood just inside the gate separating the stands from the field watching as each man stepped forward and waved to the crowd.

After several minutes of photos, the rest of the men in suits stepped off to stand near the gate where I stood as William, Clay, the announcer and a Nationals player stayed near home plate. The man announced that William would throw the first pitch, handing him a ball as William made his way toward the pitcher's mound. The Nationals player situated himself behind home plate, while Clay and the announcer stood off to the side.

William took his place on the mound and faced the plate. Without much wind-up or fanfare at all, he threw the ball towards home plate. I watched as it slowly sailed in the air and the player had to slide to the side a foot or two to catch it, slightly missing its mark. All in all, it wasn't a terrible throw, just a slow and easy one like he was playing catch. It was obvious he wasn't much of a baseball player and he didn't look to put much effort behind the action. The crowd politely applauded, and he raised his hand to them and waved as he jogged off the field and headed in my direction by the gate.

To my surprise, he came straight to me and placed a chaste kiss on my lips before pulling back and waving to the crowd again. I knew he just did it for appearances, but I couldn't help but be shocked. He *never* showed more affection in public than was necessary and I sure had not expected him to acknowledge me there more than he had to, let alone kiss me. It wasn't like it was an intense or passionate kiss, though. Quick and close-mouthed, that was definitely his style. Despite my unease, I put on a smile and acted like his attentions were the most normal thing in the world.

I glanced in Clay's direction as the announcer began to introduce him and noticed that he was staring right at me with a look of pure rage on his face. His hard eyes were penetrating me from thirty feet away, his fists clenched tightly at his sides. He looked pissed.

Is he actually mad about William's kiss? And if so, what could I do about it? It's not like I could have pushed away my fiancé in front of all these people just because he wanted a kiss. He had no right to be angry. I shifted my weight from foot to foot, uncomfortable under his furious gaze, and stared at the grass, afraid that William would see me staring back at Clay if I looked up again.

William brought his attention back to the field and listened to the announcer talk about Clay's throwing arm, while I carefully raised my eyes to Clay, trying to seem nonchalant and uninterested in the show. I was relieved to see his attention was focused back on the announcer as he answered his questions.

"So, are we going to see the old heat in that arm, Clay?" the announcer asked and angled the microphone toward him so the crowd could hear his answer.

"Well, the arm isn't what it used to be but I'll do my best," Clay answered with easy confidence.

"Oh, come on!" the announcer cajoled. "I bet you could still get your fastball up in the nineties. Let's see it!"

Clay smiled sheepishly and gave an embarrassed laugh. "I'm an old man now, Bill. I'll be lucky if I get it up to seventy!"

The announcer laughed and turned to the crowd and asked, "What do you guys think? Do you think he can do it?" There was a resounding "yes!" from the crowd followed by whoops and whistles, cheering him on.

"See, they know you can, Clay. They want to see that ninety mile-an-hour heat!" The crowd clapped and cheered even louder now, encouraging him. Clay laughed again and lifted his hat as he ran the other hand through his hair. I wondered if he really could still throw that fast. I learned during his interview earlier that he did have a great fastball back in the day but that was almost ten years ago.

Slipping the hat back on his head and smiling he said, "Alright, alright." The announcer cheered and the crowd went crazy again.

Clay took the ball and made his way toward the mound, stretching and loosening his arm along the way. He stood on the mound and leaned forward to stretch his legs a little and then stood back up but no longer had a smile on his face. Now, his face was a mask of concentration as he stared forward at the player behind the plate and dug his foot into the dirt. He bent down again to roll some dirt around in his throwing hand and rubbed the ball between his hands as he bent forward, all of his focus on the catcher's glove.

Most of the crowd was on their feet and cheering as he took his pitcher's stance. I couldn't pry my eyes off of him even if I wanted to. I forgot about William standing next to me and the reporters with their cameras behind me. I was one hundred percent focused on the man on the mound. His mask of concentration, the way his huge body was bent over, commanding the attention of the entire stadium, was one of the sexiest things I'd ever seen. He looked so strong and masculine, I just wanted to run over and jump on him. Wrap my entire body around his and never let go.

That was a nice image.

Clay brought his hands together, took a step back, bringing his knee up as his right arm pulled back in a wind-up and then flew forward with amazing speed. He released the ball like a bullet and was in the catcher's glove in the blink of an eye. In fact, if I had blinked I would have missed the whole thing.

The throw forced the catcher's weight backwards and he had to put his hand down in the dirt behind him to catch himself from completely sprawling out on the ground. The crowd went nuts and the noise got so loud one would think the game had already started. Clay jogged forward to shake the catcher's hand as the announcer rushed toward Clay, singing his praises into the microphone.

"94 miles an hour! Wow! You just threw 94 miles an hour, Clay! It doesn't seem like your arm has lost that much heat at all!"

Ever the humble man, Clay responded, "Nah, Bill, it was just the extra box of Wheaties I ate this morning." The announcer laughed and they shook hands.

Clay waved to the crowd again as he began walking toward the gate where William and I were standing. He held my gaze the entire walk over and only shifted his eyes to William when he stopped right in front of us.

I hadn't even noticed how tense William had been standing beside me for the last several minutes. I had been so entranced by Clay's performance. Now, however, I could feel the anger radiating off of him. As I looked up at his face, I could see fire behind his eyes which were locked on Clay's as he approached. *Oh no, this can't be good.* William was pissed and probably because Clay showed him up, or at the very least made the entire crowd forget he was even there. He never appreciated being made to look bad in front of the public, no matter who was to blame.

As Clay stopped in front of us, he extended his hand to William with a polite smile on his face and said in an even tone, "Well done, Callahan. This was fun." Was he purposely being sarcastic or was that just my imagination? And the way he said Callahan…it was almost with disgust. Like saying the name left a bad taste in his mouth.

After a few seconds of hesitation, William shook Clay's hand with a steel jaw and replied, "Indeed, Masterson. Though I hadn't realized it was a competition." He gritted out the words through clenched teeth.

Clay seemed to be enjoying his opponent's annoyance and gave a casual shrug. With an easy smile he responded, "Who said it was? I was just giving the crowd what they wanted. It seemed like they enjoyed it." He said the last as his eyes shifted down to mine with a mischievous glint in them, his smile transforming into one of those cocky grins.

Holy crap, he knew I'd liked that. And he was purposely baiting William with it. *What the hell is he doing? Does he want everyone to find out our secret?*

I could feel William glance at me out of the corner of my eye as I averted my gaze downward to avoid Clay's pointed one. *I mean, what is he thinking bringing attention to me in front of William? Is he insane?* I could feel William's mood escalate from simmering anger to barely contained fury. I would certainly pay in one way or another for this later. Whether his suspicions were raised by Clay's comments or not, he had to take his frustrations out on someone and I was usually the lucky winner. I had a feeling that if Clay knew the ramifications of what he said, he wouldn't have opened his mouth at all. As it was, he didn't know of William's true nature and I intended to keep it that way.

"Yes, well, we should head to our box, dear," William said to me, grabbing my elbow with minimal pressure, while still looking in Clay's direction. "Enjoy the game and the rest of your evening," he muttered to Clay, guiding me to walk up the stairs in front of him. I was careful not to meet Clay's gaze again for fear of pushing William over the edge of his control—he was almost there, I could tell—though I could feel the other man's eyes boring into my back as I ascended the stairs.

It looked like maybe this afternoon wouldn't be as relaxing as I'd hoped it would be.

CHAPTER ELEVEN

CONVERSATIONS AND REALIZATIONS

Clay

Damn, that felt good.

I hadn't thrown like that in years and I had to admit, it felt damn good. The roar of the crowd, the chanting of my name, and the sound of the ball hitting the catcher's glove was enough to make me want to rewind time for just a little bit. Back to when life seemed easier, more care-free. Back to when I didn't have as many obligations and responsibilities. Not that I'm going to start complaining about where my life is now, but it would be nice sometimes to turn back the clock for a break from the chaos.

Especially now, when my life feels like it's spinning out of control.

Maybe I shouldn't have made such a spectacle of myself, but after I saw that jackass Callahan kiss Gwen and hold her like he owned her, something in me sort of snapped. She hadn't responded to my last text, the one that made me sound like a total pansy, and it was honestly driving me crazy to not know how she felt. I probably shouldn't have sent it at all, but I couldn't help it. I had to put it out there and let her know that I hadn't been using her in the garden, that this was so much more to me than just fleeting attraction.

All I really knew for sure at this point, though, was that only one word kept running through my mind in those few minutes after I saw Callahan kiss her: *mine.*

She may not have my ring on her finger, but Gwen was *mine.* She was supposed to be with me. Somehow I just knew that, and our moment in the garden had only intensified that feeling.

And I had wanted his fucking hands off her *immediately*. Which was, of course, absolutely crazy. She was engaged to him so he had every right to touch her. I mean, they slept in the same bed for Christ's sake. It was me who didn't have the right to touch her but I couldn't help the direction of my thoughts.

I think I was slowly beginning to lose my mind every time I saw him touching any part of her, and it only made it worse now that I knew what it was like to hold her. I knew what she tasted like, what she felt like, and I hated that any other man got to enjoy that. That bastard got to see her naked. He was able to undress her. Go to bed every night with her by his side and wake up every morning to her face.

That should be *me*.

My God, I sound obsessed.

This wasn't the kind of man that I was. I don't take other men's fiancés. That nagging feeling, the one that made me feel drawn to Gwen, the one that wouldn't allow me to ignore the pull I had toward her, just wouldn't go away, though. Something didn't feel right about her engagement to Callahan but everything felt *so* right when I was near her, and I wasn't used to that. In all of my thirty-two years, I'd never had that strong of feelings for any woman, which told me something. For some inexplicable reason, I just knew that this woman was supposed to be in my life and was part of my future. And I really didn't want to slap fate in the face, if that's what this was.

After I saw them kiss, it had kind of been like an out of body experience. I'd had no control over my faculties after that. I'd gazed at him with so much fire in my eyes, I had almost expected him to burst into flames right before me. My insides were burning with the amount of rage I had coursing through my veins. My fists clenched tightly, and I grinded my teeth together so hard it had been painful.

Simply put? I wanted to knock him the hell out.

But since I couldn't have done that, and I had no other way of releasing my anger, I did the only thing I could think of that would give me back some control over the situation, even if Callahan didn't have clue what the score was. He may have her now, but if I had my way, he wouldn't for much longer.

So, what had been my objective after that kiss?

To piss William Callahan off.

And judging by the deadly scowl I saw on his face after I threw, I'd say I succeeded.

I honestly didn't know which felt better: pitching the ball and hearing the crowd go wild or seeing that look on Callahan's face and knowing that I'd gotten under his skin. It was a toss-up, really.

Though, I'd gotten pissed off all over again whenever he walked off with Gwen. Her eyes had flickered up to mine right before he carted her off, but I saw the longing there. That connection that was always there between us wasn't lost. In fact, when she looked up at me, her eyes held even more heat than usual and something else. I couldn't quite put my finger on it, but it looked something like admiration, or even adoration. Whatever it was, it made me feel like I was ten feet tall and a damn hero, so my anger eased a little after that.

That look she gave me felt better than the pitch and pissing Callahan off *combined.*

What is this woman doing to me?

That was only the five hundredth time I'd asked myself that question this week. You'd think I'd have an answer by now.

Now, I was sitting in the box that Parker had reserved for me and my family, contemplating whether or not I should storm over to Gwen and Callahan's box, throw her over my shoulder, and drag her back home with me, announcing to Callahan and the world that she was mine and that everybody had better stay the hell away.

Although I knew I would never do that, it eased my frustration slightly just entertaining the idea. If I could just talk to her it would help calm me, but I couldn't even do something as simple as that. Not with the circumstances being what they were. The entire situation was fucked up. I felt like this woman belonged with me, yet I couldn't even talk to her. I wanted to text her, but firstly, she hadn't responded to my last text. Was she possibly trying to push me away? Secondly, she was in that box with her fiancé and I didn't want him getting suspicious, which would put her in a tough spot.

You're already doing that, idiot. By pursuing her and pushing her, you're putting her in a difficult position.

I really am an idiot. And an asshole. But I simply couldn't stay away from this woman. I had tried and failed miserably.

I needed a beer. And I needed to get my mind off of Gwen for a while or I would go insane. I was at a baseball game, my family was here, and my best friend was playing, so I was going to enjoy myself one way or another.

Before I could get up out of my chair, my father plopped down in the seat beside me and handed me a fresh Budweiser. The man knew me too well.

"Thanks," I said to him, taking a deep swig and feeling my body slowly relax as the liquid ran down my throat.

"Figured you could use another," he said, glancing at me out of the corner of his eye and then took a drink of his own beer, turning his attention toward the field. "You seem a little worked up. Is it because of the whole pitching thing earlier?"

I wish that was all it was. The last thing I was going to do, though, was open up to my father about woman troubles. "No, I'm just a little stressed with the campaign and everything. Been pretty busy, you know how it is. Just hard to forget about it all whenever I actually have a chance to relax, I guess." That part was true, at least.

I could feel his eyes on me but I didn't want to look at him. He had always been able to tell when I lied to him, and I didn't feel like explaining my behavior right now. I just needed a night away from it all. Thankfully, my dad seemed to sense that and didn't explore the topic further.

"Yeah, I can understand that. Just remember, son, I'm always here if you need to talk. Alright?"

I nodded and said, "I know." And I did. While he and I may not discuss our feelings all the time, my father had always been available if I needed to unload my problems, always listening without judgment. The problem was, I didn't think he would be able to offer sound advice on my situation without judgment this time. My parents raised my sister and me to be honorable, respectable individuals, and having an affair with an engaged woman wouldn't exactly fall within either one of those categories. And I didn't want to disappoint him.

With that bit of seriousness apparently behind us, I knocked back a couple more drinks of my beer, leaned back in my chair and took in the game.

"Parker's defense has improved since last season," my dad commented and I smiled instantly.

My best friend had come from nothing and really made something of himself, and I couldn't be more proud of him. He was one of the best, if not the best, third basemen in the entire league, had one of the league's highest batting averages, and was quickly becoming one of the best players in Red Sox history.

He'd been on the injured list for almost half of last season for a torn meniscus and came back to play the last half of the season. Needless to say, his defense hadn't been great coming back after his injury. His speed and quickness hadn't been what it was before but rehab took time. Understandably, he'd been pissed at the situation, and I hated to see him in the slump he was in. He'd worked his ass of in the off-season, though, and was now looking better than ever. And the Red Sox were at the head of their division, so the postseason was looking good for them.

"Yes, it has. He says his knee hardly bothers him anymore. Who knows if that's actually true or not because you know he would never admit to being in any pain, but he's sure as hell playing like it feels better."

"That was quite the show you put on down there earlier," he said, referring to the first pitch extravaganza and not-so-subtly changing the subject in the process. I looked over at him and saw him smirking at me behind his beer bottle. *That smartass.* "Didn't know you could still throw like that did you?" His face was turning red from containing his laughter. It was starting to look painful for him.

"Shut up. I'm not that old." I couldn't help but smile too. Dad always supported my decisions, so when I'd been ready to hang up my glove and begin my career in politics, he had my back the whole way. I probably could have made it into the majors and had a pretty good career if I was lucky enough to remain injury-free, but I hadn't thought that life was for me. I loved playing, of course, but my body wasn't going to hold up forever and I had a lot that I wanted to accomplish, which I couldn't do if I was playing baseball. I've never regretted the decision, either. Even with tonight's events, I'm still happy with the course my life has taken.

So far. But one woman was really starting to make me question some of my decisions lately.

Am I really as happy as I think I am?

After the game, Parker and I went out for a few drinks at one of our favorite bars in D.C. We'd been coming here for years whenever he was in town, and it was one of the few places where Parker could go without getting harassed the entire time for autographs or pictures with fans. Since we were seen as regulars, the owners saw to it that we weren't bothered.

"So, man. What's up with you lighting it up on the mound out there and stealing my thunder tonight, huh?" asked Parker.

I knew he was just giving me shit. Parker was the most humble person I'd ever met so I knew he was joking when he said stuff like that. After growing up the way he did, way below the poverty line, one would understand if all the money and fame had gone to his head, but it hadn't, despite what some of the tabloids might occasionally say. He was not the money grubbing playboy they liked to label him as. I saw him as a man who didn't believe that life owed him anything, even though he had certainly deserved more than what life had doled out to him in his early years. He was simply achieving his dreams and enjoying his single life. He was used to ignoring all of the bullshit headlines by now, and I think they upset me more these days than they did him.

Despite his impressive six foot three frame and padded bank account, he was still the same kid I first met at the park that one afternoon when we were seven. He'd been there by himself, sitting on a bench, with his shaggy brown hair and dirty clothes that were too small for him, looking like the saddest kid in the world. My dad and I had been there playing catch and working on my swing when I saw Parker.

Me being a kid and wanting to make friends with everyone, I asked him if he wanted to play with us. He'd been really shy and would barely talk at first. His head was always downcast and his brown eyes were always wide and cautious, but he eventually inched his way over to us. We taught him everything about the game, and he seemed to love it. After that, my dad took us for ice cream and we dropped him off at his house. When my dad and I saw where he lived, we made it a point to stop by and take him to play with us whenever we had the chance.

After a few months, Parker had started to come out of his shell and started playing with me on my little league teams. He'd always had natural talent, even as a seven-year-old, and he quickly became the best kid on every team he played on. He and I became such good friends that he practically lived at our house for most of his adolescence and even spent most holidays with us.

I knew he had two older brothers, and we had always told him they were welcome to join us, but he never brought them. He wasn't a very open guy when it came to his home life and I respected that. I was guessing that whatever he endured at home was pretty bad, so I never asked about it. I just hoped that his older brothers had found a way to escape it every now and then like Parker had.

"Hey, I had to prove to everybody that I've still got it. I can't let you have all the glory." I took a drink of my beer and glanced up at the TV across from our table where the St. Louis Cardinals and Pittsburg Pirates were playing. It was nice to just kick back and have a few beers with my best friend. We hardly ever got to do it anymore, and it was exactly what I needed tonight.

"You're running for Mayor of D.C. Isn't that glory enough?"

I gave a sarcastic snort at that comment. "Yeah, it seems like too much sometimes." I tried to keep the bitter tone out of my reply but it came through regardless. Parker noticed.

He turned his chair more in my direction and gave me his full attention. "How's all that going? The campaigning," he clarified.

"It's good, actually. The polls are looking good for me and everybody's optimistic at this point. Hopefully, it will stay that way until November, but it's not going to be easy. An independent beating out a Democrat in this city is almost unheard of. Plus, I'm running against William Callahan. Everyone in this town thinks that the sun rises and sets on the Callahan's asses." This was something I could talk about: work. I could always talk about work with Parker and he could always talk about his career with me. As long as it didn't turn to my personal issues tonight, we'd be fine.

Parker nodded as he took a drink from his beer and looked as if he was contemplating something.

"What?" I asked, afraid of what was going through his head.

"If that's all going well, why do you looked like you got sucker punched in the gut?" He narrowed his eyes at me as he asked the question.

Dammit, am I that transparent? First my dad and now Parker? Have I worn my emotions on my sleeve my entire life and never realized it?

"Nothing, man. Just tired, I guess. It's been a long couple of weeks." I was trying to deflect him as best as I could because I really didn't want to ruin my good mood by talking about my relationship, or non-relationship, problems.

"You know I'm not buying that, right? I've known you for over twenty-five years, Clay. What's going on?"

I gave an exasperated sigh. This was not exactly going where I wanted it to. "Did you turn into a woman recently and forget to tell me?"

He shook his head at me and gave me a *you can't bullshit me so cut the crap* look. "You don't have to be a dick, man. I'm just asking because you look like shit."

He's right. I'm being an asshole.

I scrubbed my hands down my face and hung my head for a few seconds while I figured out what I was going to say. Before I could say anything, though, Parker caught on and chimed in.

"Don't tell me it's a woman." He said it in a chiding tone, almost reprimanding.

And it just got personal. *Perfect.*

But maybe I could actually use some advice on the matter. I still didn't want to confess the entire story, but I could provide enough details to give him the general idea of my predicament.

Well, here it goes.

I couldn't help but laugh, disbelievingly. We were now going to discuss the precise thing I wanted to avoid. "Jesus, is it that obvious?"

Parker laughed. The bastard laughed like it was the funniest damn thing in the world. "Clay Masterson all bent out of shape over a woman. I never thought I'd see the day. This calls for another round." He flagged down the waitress and asked for two more beers.

"It's not funny, dude. The woman drives me crazy. I can't get her out of my head."

"I'm sorry. It's just that this is coming from the guy who never lets himself get too close to any woman and now you're hung up on one." He laughed again behind his mug. I was so close to tipping it up and letting it spill all over his face. "So, who is she?"

This is where it got complicated. "Um, just someone. You don't know her."

"Is this some sort of secret or something?" He acted surprised and I couldn't say that I blamed him. During all our years of friendship, there had never been anything that we couldn't discuss with one another. We didn't keep secrets from each other and if we did, they didn't stay secret for long. Unfortunately, this was a secret that even Parker couldn't know until I figured some things out.

"Sort of. It's a complicated situation. We can't exactly announce ourselves to the public right now." It sounded vague but there wasn't much more I could say without revealing too much.

"You mean because of the campaign?"

Not really. Sort of. "Something like that."

"Okay, so you've got to keep things on the down low for a while. I get it. So, what's the problem?" There was a group of three girls, probably college age, trying to get his attention from a couple tables over, but he didn't seem to notice or care. His olive skin, big brown eyes, and toothpaste commercial smile never failed to attract the ladies. I'm sure the multimillion dollar salary he had didn't hurt either.

How to explain it? "There's just some other obstacles in the way of us actually having a relationship, and she's not sure if she's ready to deal with all that. Hell, I'm not sure if I'm ready to deal with that."

Am I? Am I ready to take on her fiancé? Her parents? The media?

"Are you worried about how it's going to affect your campaign image? Or your ratings in the polls or something?"

I immediately got defensive at that. "Hell no. Sure, I want to get into office, but I don't care about any of that when it comes to her. I'm more concerned about how it would affect her if our relationship was made public. There are more people involved in our situation than just us, and there could be some negative repercussions if we don't handle it carefully. It's her image I'm worried about. The last thing I want to do is hurt her."

157

"Christ, she's not a Democrat is she?" he joked. Although I wasn't able to laugh at the situation, I appreciated that he was trying to lighten my mood.

I gave him a look. "Hilarious, but not helping."

He smiled and put his hands up in front of him. "Alright, alright. Just let me ask you this. How much is she worth? Is she worth going through all that hassle, going up against all those people?"

Is she? That was the big question. The one I had to answer before I went any further with this liaison.

It didn't take me long to figure it out, though. I didn't even have to debate with myself. I'd been debating over the issue for the last month and a half. I've known the answer for a while.

I looked him in the eyes and said in a serious, no-nonsense tone, "Yes. She is."

He nodded his head, looking satisfied with my answer. "Then here's my advice. Not that I'm an expert in love or anything, and it's hard to know what's really going on when you won't give me all the details, but I know people and I know you."

He paused and stared down into his beer for a minute, looking like he was either lost in his own thoughts or just trying to figure out what to say next. He brushed his dark hair out of his face—he still preferred to wear it a little longer, almost touching his shoulders—as he pondered his words. After several seconds, he looked back up at me.

"Go after her, man. Make sure she knows that you're willing to fight for her and willing to make whatever it is between you two work. If she hears that you can be strong in the situation, she'll be more likely to trust you and be strong herself. Women need to rely on us. As much as they might try to deny it, they do. Make sure she knows how you feel and that you're not going to back down."

I'd never heard him open up like this before. He never discussed intimate details about his family with me, and I respected that because I knew it was a really sore subject for him. He'd been through a lot. So, hearing this from him was a bit of a surprise but everything he said made sense, all of it. I knew Gwen wanted to rely on me because, though she never said as much, she didn't feel like she could rely on anyone else. And I wanted to be that man for her. I *needed* to be that man. But the uncertainty of what her reaction would be if I completely put myself out there created a seed of worry.

"And what if she says no and decides she can't do it?"

"Then at least you can say that you gave her everything that you could. If you do everything you can now, then you won't have regrets down the road and blame yourself for not doing more." He said the last in such a sober tone and with such a somber look on his face, I wondered if what he said was coming from personal experience.

Maybe we have more secrets than I thought.

Then, the look was wiped from his face as quickly as it came, and I had to stop to make sure that I hadn't imagined the whole thing. Deciding to file that information away for another time, I flashed a grin and chugged the rest of my beer, trying to loosen up the moment.

"How in the hell did you get so wise, Cruz?"

The cocky smirk was back. "You're just now realizing that? I've always been smarter than you. Remember that." There was the smartass, care-free friend I knew.

The rest of the night was easy going and lacked any more intense conversations. We caught up on baseball, Parker's recovery, my family, and future holidays, since Parker usually spent them with us when he could. In other words, it was a refreshing reprieve from my current reality, which I would have to go back to bright and early the next morning.

On my drive home, I thought about the conversation we had and what Parker had said. He was absolutely right. If I was willing to fight, then I had to make sure that Gwen knew it. I went through all of my options then made some plans.

As soon as I got through my front door, I pulled out my phone and sent a text.

CHAPTER TWELVE

THE MATCH AND THE FLAME

Gwen

I was bracing myself for a fierce encounter with William when we returned home after the game, but what happened left me utterly shocked.

He left me alone.

He didn't say one word to me from the time we left the stadium to the moment when he walked back out the front door, leaving to go wherever he went most nights. I was expecting him to yell at me like he often did for no reason. Or to get rough and use me as a way of taking back some control while releasing his aggression at the same time.

But, no. Instead he completely ignored me. Not that I was complaining. Hell, I was practically rejoicing. But his behavior also unnerved me. He'd never done that before, just ignored and left me without a word, giving no hint to his thoughts or intentions, and I didn't know what to think about it. It honestly worried me more than his violent side because at least when he was yelling I knew what to expect and I was mostly prepared for it.

This side of him I'd never seen before and it felt sort of like I was headed into battle unarmed. Clay must have really gotten to him this evening and it may have caused him to consider changing his tactics up. Perhaps he hadn't seen Clay as legitimate competition before but he was rethinking that assessment now, I was sure. I definitely wouldn't be letting my guard down around him anytime soon with this change in behavior, but I was also going to enjoy this evening by myself and not dwell on dreary thoughts.

I went to my study and worked on the new novel I was starting on, the ideas for which had been swimming around in my head for weeks, and spent a good two hours creating the storyline. Satisfied with what I'd accomplished, I went upstairs to change into my swimsuit. Half an hour in the Jacuzzi sounded like absolute paradise.

I poured myself a glass of wine and grabbed a towel out of the pool house before I eased my body down under the steaming water. The powerful jets and heat of the water had already started to work wonders on my muscles as I settled myself onto the carved-out bench along the wall. As soon as I leaned my head back onto the edge of the Jacuzzi, my phone beeped with a text message.

Irrationally, my heart skipped a beat with the hope that it would be the only person I actually cared to talk to right now. I grabbed it and looked at the screen.

It was *him*. And it didn't take two seconds after I saw his name for that smile to come to my face. The one that made me look like a Cheshire cat, it was so wide. I knew I was acting like a giddy fifteen-year-old girl, waiting by the phone for her boyfriend to call. It may have been so wrong to feel that way about a man who was not my fiancé but, again, I didn't care.

Clay: *Go for a run at the park on Tuesday. 8am. Southwest corner.*

Oh, boy. Today was Saturday, so Tuesday was only three days from now. I knew responding to him was probably a bad idea. I should just delete the message and pretend like it never happened like I did before. And meeting him at the park? It was one thing to talk to him over the phone, but to actually meet him on purpose, in public? That was taking things to another level, and even though I felt beyond compelled to be near this man, I didn't know if I was ready for that next step.

Me: *I don't think that's a good idea.*

It didn't take long for his response.

Clay: *I think it is. It wouldn't be the first time we "ran into each other" at the park. This time it will just be on purpose.*

What was I supposed to tell him? I should give him a flat-out *no* but whenever I moved my fingers over the keys to type that answer out, I couldn't. I didn't want to disappoint him and, more importantly, I *wanted* to see him again. Alone. Just the two of us.

I bit my lip, worrying about what to do. Could I do this? Could I completely ignore all the warning signs currently flashing in my head, telling me this was the worst idea ever? Could I, for once, do something that was totally selfish and one hundred percent for me and nobody else?

Me: *I don't know...*

Clay: *It will be fine, trust me. I have to see you. I'll keep bothering you until you say yes. Don't doubt my persistence.*

Clay: *Please.*

Ah, hell. That damn please again. When he put it that way, sounding as desperate as I felt, maybe one quick meeting wouldn't be so terrible. We could just casually run into each other and it be as innocent as the first time it had happened.

Yes, but you've made out with him since then and you know that's all you'll be thinking about once you see him in person.

That voice in my head needed to shut up. I wasn't asking for its opinion.

But since what it said made sense, I decided I'd have to give myself time to consider this and what it would mean. More importantly, whether or not it would ultimately be worth it and if I would be ready for the consequences should something go wrong.

Me: *Let me think about it and I'll let you know. Okay?*

It look him a little longer to reply that time.

Clay: *Fair enough.*

As soon as I read Clay's last text, I proceeded to delete all of the rest. I hated to because I wanted evidence that he'd actually contacted me, letting me know this was real, but I couldn't risk William seeing them on my phone. Every now and then he would take my phone and look through my calls and texts, I guess making sure I wasn't contacting anyone I wasn't supposed to. I had to be very careful from this point on if Clay and I were going to be in contact with each other.

I would have to make my decision by Monday night at the latest whether or not I would do this. Right now, though, I was just going to have a gloriously relaxing soak in my hot tub and clear my mind of everything I didn't want in it.

This, of course, meant that the only things on my mind while I luxuriated in the hot water were images of Clay's blue eyes, his amazing lips, his gorgeous smile, and his incredibly strong arms and hard chest. My head became consumed with thoughts of how his hands felt on me and what would happen the next time he got them back on me, *if* he got them back on me. The thought sent a shiver down my spine and traveled all the way to my toes and fingers, making them tingle. Then, as I sat in the hot tub with the water heating my entire body, I did something that I hadn't done in a long time.

I touched myself.

And I imagined it was Clay Masterson's hands on me the entire time.

My mother had scheduled dress fittings at some of the top designers in the D.C. area for the next morning and afternoon. So, I met her at the first store at 10:30, ready for the worst. She had chosen all of the designers and had booked the appointments. I hadn't had a choice in the matter. I was hoping that this would be a stress-free experience, but that was like wishing for a pet unicorn: ridiculous and unrealistic. I just felt like there was a dark cloud that had settled over me as soon as I'd left the house that morning, as if a downpour was going to hit me at any moment.

To say that I was less than enthusiastic would be a drastic understatement. I wanted to be excited but couldn't be for two reasons: 1) I was marrying Satan, and 2) it was almost a guarantee that my mother and I wouldn't agree on anything. The one thing that most girls got truly excited about when it came to planning their weddings was the dress. We wanted to look and feel beautiful, so if I got my way with anything in relation to this God forsaken wedding, I wanted it to be my dress.

My mother was already in the shop, picking out options and shoving them at the sales woman to put inside my dressing room by the time I walked through the doors.

My mother turn her head in my direction and, with a curt, business-like tone, said, "Oh, there you are." She quickly turned away and went right back to perusing the racks. "I've already got some dresses in your room, so you can go on back and get started. Clarice will help with the zippers and buttons."

"Uh, I wanted to look for some too, Mother," I replied in an even but firm tone, letting her know that I was perfectly serious about this and wouldn't budge.

She looked back at me with slightly narrowed eyes and muttered, "Fine but hurry up. We've got to be at Karen's by 12:30," she snapped, referring to the next fitting appointment.

I went through most of the racks fairly quickly because I knew what I was looking for and it wasn't what I was seeing. Poof. I did not favor the princess, ball gown look, nor did I think that I could pull it off. I wanted something more form-fitted, while at the same time flattering and elegant. I loved the vintage and modern mix that was coming back, and I was partial to lace. I was thinking something with a keyhole back, capped sleeves, a full lace overlay and a medium-length train to complete the look.

Okay, so yes, I'd thought about it a time or two. What girl didn't? But the reason I was so specific about the design and the reason I was so determined to find that exact one was because my grandmother wore one almost exactly like it when she married my grandfather.

I had seen countless pictures of my grandparent's wedding when I was young, and I immediately fell in love with her dress. It was beautiful and classic and she had looked stunning in it. She had kept it in a garment bag in her closet over the years and I loved when she let me put it on and we would pretend it was my wedding. We would paper machete a bouquet of flowers and she would throw rice in the air as she hummed *The Bridal March.*

I wanted to look as beautiful on my wedding day as she had on hers, so I always told her that I was going to wear a dress like hers. Her face would light up with so much pride and love whenever I talked about it, and she even told me that I could have her dress whenever she was gone. So when she died, I had expected for her to leave it to me.

But I never got it. Nothing was said about it and nobody knew anything about it. I went looking for it myself but it was gone from her closet and was nowhere else in the house to be found. I had no idea what had happened to it and I was devastated. Not only did I love that dress but it also reminded me of so many cherished afternoons with my grandmother, which were the only times I could really remember ever being carefree enough to actually have fun in my childhood.

But I never found it.

I ended up finding three dresses that looked close to what I was imagining and took them back to my room. I opened the door that had my name on it and was appalled by what was waiting for me inside: poof. It was everywhere. It was like a conglomeration of tool, taffeta, chiffon, and ruffles that had been regurgitated all over my dressing room. There were sequins and rhinestones and trains longer than Princess Di's. They were pretentious and gaudy and I hated all of them. My mom chose all of them solely because they screamed "Look at me, look at me! Look at how much money I have and how important I am!"

Basically? It was my worst nightmare.

The clouds opened up. *Here comes the downpour.*

We were at our third and final shop of the day, and I was so strung out that I was surprised I hadn't killed my mother in a blind rage. I wasn't sure that any amount of wine I was going to consume later would help ease this kind of tension.

I had tried on every dress my mother had chosen and looked hideous in all of them. And I said as much. My mother, of course, ignored me and found several that she preferred. Despite her looks of disgust, I tried on the ones I liked and found a couple that I adored. She made it known how simple and plain they all looked and "unbefitting" of a McKindry bride.

The last shop we hit I tried one on that I had picked out and instantly fell in love. It was "the one" and I knew it right away. It had everything I wanted: the keyhole back, the capped sleeves, all covered in lace. As I admired myself in it through the mirror, I found myself wondering if he would like it. Only the *he* I was picturing wasn't my fiancé. It was Clay. I was imagining what Clay would think of me in this dress and how he would look at me as I walked down the aisle towards him instead of William.

Wow, I really am turning back into a fifteen-year-old girl. I mentally berated myself for that stupid thought because I knew very well that that would never happen. Trying on wedding dresses was a dangerous thing because it put stupid thoughts into your head that didn't belong there, *ever*. And although I didn't want to waste wearing this beautiful dress for William, I also didn't know if I was ever going to have another wedding. If my parents and William had their way, I wouldn't. It would be William forever. So, if that was the case and this was the only wedding dress I was ever going to wear, I at least wanted to love it. It would probably be my only pleasant memory of the day.

I think my mother could sense my excitement over the dress because she merely scowled and walked out of the room. She had always resented my relationship with her mother because it was the complete opposite of the one they had had with each other. My grandmother had tried so hard with her over the years, but money and power had become more important to my mother than family bonds. They never saw eye to eye, much like me and my mom, and I knew that jealously ate at her whenever we had started becoming so close.

It was obvious she hated that I wanted my dress to look so much like her mother's. In fact, I had always had my suspicions that my mother was behind the case of the missing wedding dress and for whatever reason, she didn't want me to have it. It wouldn't surprise me that one of the few things I wanted of hers, my mother would hide from me. At least, I hoped she was hiding it and hadn't destroyed it or anything. Although, I wouldn't put it past her if she had.

A few minutes later, I was stepping out of the room in my normal clothes, with the dress in my arms, as I tried to find the sales woman who was helping me so I could have them hold onto it for me. I knew I wanted this dress, but this was only the first day of fittings, so I would appease my mother by going to more shops and try more on. I could just come back here later without her and buy it.

As I neared the front desk, I could see her speaking to the sales woman and handing over her credit card, which confused me. We hadn't mentioned that we wanted to buy one yet, so why would she need a credit card? She straightened her shoulders as I approached her, looking like she was ready for a fight. *Oh, no. This can't be good.*

"What are you doing?" I asked in the most authoritative voice I could manage.

"I'm buying your wedding dress," she replied nonchalantly, as if she were discussing something as commonplace as the weather.

"What? You're buying this for me?" I asked, disbelievingly, as I held out the dress in my arms. I was *so* not expecting this. That she would actually give in to something that I wanted.

The cold laugh she released at my question wiped the astonishment from my mind and immediately put me back on alert. She shook her head at me, like she couldn't believe I would even suggest such a thing.

"Of course not. I'm buying that first one you tried on here. It was my favorite by far."

Every muscle in my body froze and I stopped breathing.

She did not.

Oh. Hell. No.

She loved the first one so much because it was without a doubt the worst one I'd tried on all day. The layers and layers of tool under the skirt made the whole thing stick out about three feet all the way around. The bodice was a corset-style and was covered in sequins and rhinestones. It was so tight that it pushed my breasts up practically to my chin and was unbearably uncomfortable. It also had the heaviest train of any dress I had tried on. Between the skirt and the train, I probably wouldn't be able to even fit through a doorway. I might as well make a sign that said "Wide Load" and pin it to my ass. It was one of the tackiest things I had ever seen in my life and it was going to be a cold day, a sub-Arctic day in hell before I walked down the aisle in that thing.

I'm not sure if what happened next could technically be classified as a Bridezilla moment since I'd been building up to it since I was a kid. And since any other girl probably would have reacted the same way if their mother was a straight-up bitch.

But my claws definitely came out.

"No, Mother. I don't want that dress. I want this one." I paused to make sure I had her attention as I spoke the next words slowly in order to get my point across. "I'm getting this one."

"Don't be silly. That one wasn't at all appropriate." She spoke like she was talking to a five-year- old who was begging for candy.

"I don't care if it's not appropriate!" I shouted, not caring how loud I was being or who heard me. The thread that I'd been holding onto, clinging to, had broken. My fury was bubbling up to the surface and was about to blow with a force that I wouldn't be able to control.

A look of rage took over her face as she leaned into me and whispered harshly, "Keep your voice down. You're making a scene." Her voice was low but it was sharp and angry. *Well, join the club.* "And you will wear this one because I said so. Your father and I are paying for this wedding, so you'll do whatever we tell you to. No discussions."

Well, that did it.

The volcano had finally erupted and hell was being unleashed.

"No, Mother. I'm not going to keep my voice down because I'm not going to wear that horribly ugly dress. The only reason I'm going through with this is because you basically said that you would ruin me if I didn't. If you and Dad want me to go through with this wedding, then you will allow me to wear whatever damn dress I want, without comment. If you don't, I have absolutely no problem cancelling the whole thing and telling all of you to go to hell."

With that last parting shot, I found the sales woman, who'd been frozen in place with eyes as big as saucers during our tirade, and asked her to hold my dress for me. I would have bought it right then, but I needed to get away from my mother as fast as humanly possible before I did something I couldn't take back, like slap her.

I stomped out of that shop without a backwards glance and marched down the sidewalk for a few minutes, trying to calm down, before I eventually flagged down a cab and rattled off my home address. On the way home, I thought about everything that had happened the last few days. The Nationals game, Clay's text last night, everything that happened today.

After contemplating all of these events and my feelings towards them, I came to a conclusion and it was this: *Screw it.*

I was so angry and so sick of having almost no control over my life, I decided to take advantage of this opportunity to do something just for the sole pleasure of doing it. I didn't care about the consequences or how I would feel afterwards.

I wanted this. There was no *but* this time. I wanted it. I wanted him and that was it. So I whipped out my phone and sent a text.

Me: *Tuesday. The park. 8am. See you there.*

This was either going to be the best or worst thing that I'd ever done for myself.

And I was praying that it would be the former.

CHAPTER THIRTEEN

SECRET MEETINGS AND WHISPERED PROMISES

Gwen

My heart was beating a mile a minute. I wasn't sure if it was from the anticipation of seeing Clay or from the fear of someone possibly seeing us together. Regardless, my breathing exercises to try and slow my heart rate were not working at all, and I made a mental note to find a new yoga instructor. Her methods were completely ineffective.

I was stretching out my limbs in a grassy area off the path by the front entrance to the park, behaving like I always did when I came for a run but at the same time keeping a watch out for Clay. He said southwest corner so I was assuming that's where he would meet me, but I wanted to be alert at all times so he didn't catch me off guard.

Although it was summer, the sun hadn't risen above the buildings and trees yet so it was still a little chilly out. I knew, though, that I'd warm up as soon as I started moving so I hadn't brought a jacket. I wore my racer back pink Nike tank with black spandex capri pants and my favorite gray and black running shoes. My hair was pulled back in a ponytail and my black iPod arm band was strapped to my upper right arm.

I could be honest and admit that I wanted to look good for Clay, at least as good as one can look when running. My top and pants clung to my curves and I may have put a dash of mascara on for good measure. I knew how ridiculous it was. I was acting like a preteen with her first crush, but I didn't seem to have complete control of my person when it came to this man.

When I felt warmed up enough, I started jogging on the same path I was on when we first ran into each other. Since it was still early, there weren't that many people in the park. There were some other runners on the path and a few people sitting on benches drinking coffee and reading the newspaper.

As my muscles started to loosen up, I could feel myself start to relax and my mind cleared, giving me a momentary respite from my current worries and stress. Running was therapeutic for me and usually renewed my energy. I just wished I could do it more often.

Avicii blasted through my headphones as I came to the southwest corner of the park and I began looking around. Whether I was supposed to be looking for Clay or something else, I didn't know. This area of the park was wooded with trees lining the path on the right side and, in some areas, on both sides of the path. As I got closer to the more heavily wooded section, I saw him. He was bent down in a runner's stretch beside the path, near the trees. He looked like any other runner out for a jog, warming up his muscles.

He wore a plain white t-shirt and black running shorts with white stripes down the sides, similar to what he wore the first time I saw him running there. I took in his tanned, athletic form, from his large, muscled arms to his toned, powerful legs and practically drooled. I appreciated the sight the first time I ran into him at the park, but now that I knew what it felt like to be held by those arms and what that hard body felt like to rub up against, my core instantly clenched. Just the sight of him made me hyperaware of all of my bodily sensations. He was that beautiful.

As if he could hear my thoughts, he lifted his head and looked straight at me. His eyes pierced mine, gifting me with that same hungry look that he had in the garden. With his body bent down, his muscles flexing, and his gaze locked on mine, he looked almost animalistic, feral even. Waiting to pounce on his prey like a lion. Warmth spread throughout my entire body at the sight, and I could feel that my underwear were already soaked through. *I haven't even spoken to him yet!*

His mouth formed into a half smirk as if he knew exactly the effect he was having on me and I was sure he did. No doubt I wasn't the first female that had literally tripped over herself at the mere sight of him. I knew Clay was very much aware of how women responded to him, but he never flaunted it. He was confident but not arrogant, and from what I had always seen and heard of him, he always treated women with the utmost respect, and I certainly respected a man like that.

He stood up from his stretch as I slowed down to approach him. I was unbelievably nervous and had about a thousand butterflies fluttering around in my stomach, but I couldn't stop my mouth from curving up into a huge smile as soon as he flashed his pearly whites at me.

"Hey," he said when I stopped and stood a few feet in front of him.

"Hi." I was a little winded but I was pretty sure that my heavy breathing had nothing to do with the jog.

"I'm glad you came." His voice was deep and husky and was probably the most soothing sound I had ever heard.

"I am too." It was the truth. In that moment, looking up at him and being close enough to breathe in his delicious scent, I was so, *so* glad that I had come. No pun intended. Because I hadn't…yet.

His eyes slowly roamed up and down my body, his pupils dilating and his nostrils flaring. "You look good." His voice came out even lower and my face heated. I wasn't yet used to his attentions, but it felt amazing to be noticed and appreciated.

I allowed my eyes to peruse over his body again, memorizing every ripple of muscle. The words flew out of my mouth before I had time to think. "So do you."

His jaw clenched at my words and his head jerked around, searching the area. When he saw no one on the path near us, he took three long strides toward me, grabbed my wrist and started walking toward the trees, pulling me behind him and mumbling "come on."

"Where are we going?" I asked him, my breath coming faster at the thought of him wanting to be alone with me again. I honestly didn't care where we were going, just as long as he didn't stop touching me.

"Just follow me," was his only response.

We were walking into the wooded area along a small footpath that I hadn't noticed before. I looked behind us and was surprised that the foliage was dense enough that we couldn't be seen from the main path anymore. We were completely hidden now.

My breathing kicked up a notch.

We were alone again.

Clay stopped walking all of a sudden, whipping around with a fierce look in his eyes, and pulled me closer to him. My body was now pressed up against his, his breathing coming out just as erratic as mine was.

I looked up and met his eyes as he lowered his head and whispered, "I missed you."

My breath hitched at his confession but before I could respond, he crushed his lips down onto mine. He tasted just as incredible as before, maybe even more so and it sent a jolt of need down below my belly. It felt like years since I'd last felt him and I didn't want this to ever stop.

But I was ashamed to say that I suddenly had a moment of panic. My mind reverted back to dark thoughts of someone catching us, demolishing both of our lives with a single headline in the *Post*: "*Callahan's Fiancé has Affair with Competition, McKindry Downfall Inevitable.*" In a single second, I forgot all my vows to do something for me and enjoy being with someone who actually seemed to care. My vision was clouded with flashes of William lashing out in a homicidal rage at me and Clay, and all of a sudden I didn't feel as brave and confident as I had the other day when I'd yelled at my mother. I shrunk inside myself and allowed all of my fears to crawl back to the forefront of my mind.

Before I even registered what I was doing, I raised my hands to Clay's chest and pushed him away from me, though it killed me to. I wanted nothing more than to pull him back and give him everything I had, but I couldn't command my body to do it. He stumbled back, taking his delectable lips with him, with a surprised look on his face.

I hated seeing his forehead furrowed in both hurt and confusion, his eyes staring at me asking so many silent questions, but I tried to ignore both or I'd never get the words out. "I don't know if I can do this, Clay," I said, my voice trembling.

"Yes you can, Gwen. You told me in the garden you felt the pull between us—"

"Maybe that shouldn't have happened," I interrupted. I was such a coward. *What am I doing?* I didn't want this. I didn't want to tell him no. *Stop telling him no!*

"You don't mean that," he said with a determined edge in his voice. "I know what I felt when we kissed," he continued before I could say anything more. "I could feel how bad you wanted me, I know that was real. It's real for me, too, and I hope you know that." He paused to take a deep breath. "I know you're engaged and normally, I would never pursue a taken woman, but it's different with you, Gwen. I know it probably sounds cliché but I have never felt like this, ever, and I can't ignore the nagging voice in my head that's telling me to be close to you. I can't explain it and I know it doesn't make any sense, but something is telling me that I'm supposed to be with you, that we're supposed to be together." He bowed his head then and thrust his hands through his hair in frustration, acting like he didn't know what to say next.

I lost all semblance of thought with that last statement. I was both shocked and relieved that he felt the exact same thing that I was feeling, that maybe it wasn't just a ridiculous crush and I wasn't crazy. It put me even more at ease that he seemed just as confused and lost about the situation as I did. He always seemed so confident and self-assured. But in that moment, he didn't look like he had an answer and I could tell that didn't happen often. It bothered him immensely.

Maybe all I'd really needed was reassurance from him. Reassurance that he was just as scared as I was about all of this, but he was willing to try it if I was. His career would suffer if it was revealed that he was having an affair with an engaged woman and the fiancé of D.C.'s golden boy, no less. So, he had just as much to lose as me if we were ever discovered. But he was willing to risk it all anyway, for me.

For me. A light bulb clicked on in my head at the thought and suddenly everything seemed so clear. Everything was finally starting to make some sense and my fears from a moment ago were instantly replaced with overpowering elation. Clay was doing this, risking everything, for *me*. And maybe it took me longer than it should have to figure this out, but better late than never, right? The fact that he was still willing to enter into a relationship with me despite all of it, and the fact that he was baring his soul to me, meant more than I could say. It was precisely the push I needed to put everything else aside and allow myself to become totally consumed by the need I felt for this man. I was being such an emotional rollercoaster, I knew it. But now I knew, without a doubt, what I was going to do.

I opened my mouth to respond to him, but before I could, he blurted out, "I mean, is it just one-sided here? Are you not feeling this at all? Am I just crazy?" He was pacing in front of me and looking down at the ground as he ranted. "Because you're all I've been able to think about and I seriously don't know what to do. Everything in my life feels so upside down, but when I'm around you, it just feels right. I know it should feel wrong but it doesn't. It's easy to be near you, which tells me that this just can't be wrong."

I almost wanted to laugh at how disheveled he looked. His hair was sticking up in every direction from running his hands through it. His hands were now forming fists at his sides and he was walking briskly back and forth like a caged animal. He looked manic. I just had to stop and admire the humor of the situation. Here we were, two reasonable, usually responsible, adults with both of our lives feeling like they were spinning out of control. And we were both losing our minds all because of the other person.

Seeing him practically break apart in front of me somehow gave me the absolution to say what I'd wanted to for weeks. In that moment, I forgot everything that I was probably supposed to say and listened to the part of me that I'd locked away from the world. The part I realized I now wanted to share with this man. My heart.

Because he was right. Neither one of us were capable of ignoring this thing between us and I felt like we weren't supposed to ignore it. Like him, I had this overwhelming sense that this man was my future, and I was done denying myself from experiencing a little bit of happiness.

With my decision made, I walked forward and stopped only inches in front of him. He didn't look at me until I brought my hand up and cupped his cheek in a gentle, soothing touch. He leaned his head into it, trying to feel more of it. His blue eyes communicated so much need when he met my gaze that there was no way I could walk away from him.

"Hey," I murmured, moving closer to him, needing to be closer to him. "It doesn't feel wrong to me either. I don't know how we're going to do this, but I think I'm ready to see how it goes if you are." I was working up more and more strength the more I spoke. "I can't guarantee that I'll be able to give you what you want but I want to try." I nervously bit my lip as I waited for his reply.

He sucked in a deep breath and exhaled with the widest smile I had ever seen on his face, looking beyond relieved. "Look, I'll be happy with any part of you that I can get because I know this won't be easy. I know you have another part of your life that I'll have to respect and I promise to do so because I also know that you're worth it." He stepped toward me and framed my face in his hands, his eyes softening as he caressed my cheeks with his thumbs. "We'll be careful and take it slow, okay?" I nodded and licked my lips in an anxious gesture. His eyes moved to my lips at the movement, his jaw hardening. I saw the telltale sign of desire in his features, which was confirmed by the bulge in his shorts that I felt slowly hardening. "But I can't talk anymore right now."

Without another word, he sealed his lips to mine in an urgent, bruising kiss that I loved. I didn't try to resist him this time. I threw myself into the kiss, wrapping my arms around his neck and sinking into his embrace, his arms squeezing me tightly to him. I'd wanted to feel this again so bad. A slight whimper left my mouth as he deepened the kiss, his mouth becoming more desperate and hungry, his tongue tangling wildly with mine, attacking every inch of my mouth.

His hands started roaming over my body in frantic movements, like he had to touch me everywhere at once. I felt both hands grip my ass and lift me up. I took the hint and wrapped my legs around his waist while he walked forward until my back was pressed up against a tree.

I loved his strength and the ease with which he held me up, as if I weighed nothing. I felt safe in his arms, which went a long way in my world considering I felt the complete opposite when I was anywhere near

William. I hadn't realized until that moment how much I craved that feeling, how much I needed it. It only made Clay more of a temptation.

One of his arms was braced on the tree near my head while the other grasped under my ass, holding me up. I gasped, moaning as he took my bottom lip between his teeth and bit down, which Clay responded to with a deep groan of his own. His mouth moved down my jawline, traveling along my neck. His warm breath was giving me goose bumps, his soft kisses and wet tongue intensifying the building ache in my core. He seemed ravenous and I was following right behind him into the abyss.

I needed relief. Soon.

"God, you feel good," he murmured against my skin. His voice sounded strained, desire and need evident in his words. "We're going to finish what we didn't get to last time."

"Oh my God, yes," I whispered back. I was desperate for that and I was prepared to tell him. I didn't want to filter my thoughts with him anymore. He was the only person in my life who I felt I could be completely honest with. Who would still accept me no matter what.

"I want more of you, Gwen. I need more." He was breathing harder, his words spoken between harsh pants as his mouth moved back up my neck and captured mine in another blinding kiss.

I needed more too, so much more. I tugged on his hair at the back of his neck, knowing he loved it when I did that, bringing him closer to me, while my other hand moved down to grasp his tight backside, bringing his lower half in closer proximity to mine. *Ah, there.* That was the friction I needed. Without thinking, I began to move my hips, grinding my sex right up against his erection that was growing harder by the second. A deep, almost beastly, sound emanated from Clay at the sensation as he reciprocated, thrusting his hips in return, a movement that started off slow and sensual but was quickly becoming frenzied.

Clay

I could feel Gwen's heat rubbing against me through our clothes, and I knew she was wet for me. I was hard as steel from the thought of taking her right here against this tree, but as demanding as my body was for a release provided by this woman, I wouldn't let it happen. Our first time would be in a bed, a place where she deserved and where I would be able to savor every inch of her body all night long.

Even though I knew that she wanted this as much as I did, I also knew I was putting her in a very difficult position and she deserved to be treated with the utmost care. I wanted to show her pleasure, wanted to show her how special and appreciated she was and just how much her giving in to me like this meant to me. I wanted to show her what it should be like with a man, what it *will* be like with *me*. I knew she didn't let a lot of people in, but for some inexplicable reason, she was letting me in and I knew it was a big deal for her. She was giving me an opportunity and I was determined to not screw it up. I would not allow her to regret trusting me like this.

Her breathing was heavy and she could barely get the words out. "I know. I need more, too," she gasped as I hit the spot where she most needed pressure. "Ahh, there. Right there, Clay."

I could tell she was close to her pleasure so I quickened my movements and thrust harder. If we'd already been together before this, I'd be impaling her on this tree right now. Although I was going to walk away from this experience with one of the worst cases of blue balls in history, I refused to stop until she was sated and satisfied. At least as satisfied as we could manage in a public park.

"Yeah?" I was looking down at her passion-glazed face while she continued to writhe against me. She was beautiful beyond words every time I saw her, but with her eyes closed, lips parted, and body shuddering in the throes of desire, she was absolutely stunning. "You like that? Feel good?"

"God, *yes*. Please, please," she breathed. She kept chanting the last word over and over like that was all her brain could process.

"Yeah, that's right. Give it to me." I needed to be the one to send her over the edge almost as much as her body needed to plunge over it. I needed to feel her body give in to me. It was part of that possessive, primal urge inside me that desperately wanted this woman to belong to me. I wanted to own her body. I wanted to be in charge of her pleasure. *Only* me. "I want to see you come for me, Gwen. Give in to me."

Even though I'd already felt her bare sex and had my fingers inside her in the garden, I honestly hadn't planned on taking it that far again this time. I didn't want to spook her and have her run away from me again, so pleasuring her against a tree wasn't exactly what I'd had in mind when I'd asked her to meet me. I'd wanted to talk to her and sort some things out.

Obviously, though, I had a problem keeping my hands to myself around this woman and I certainly wasn't opposed to what we were doing. When I had started kissing her, it was really because I hadn't been able to go another second without savoring her taste again. I hadn't even cared that I probably sounded pussy-whipped with what I was confessing. She felt so incredibly good that it made it all worth it.

I had expected her to fight me. She was going to deny it as much as she could and try to convince herself that she didn't want this, that we couldn't allow it to happen. I knew because I'd been fighting the same thoughts in my head for weeks, but I was done with it. This connection was more powerful than I could handle and I was exhausted from trying to fight it.

But even more importantly, I had come to realize that when I was with Gwen, I felt happy. Before her I hadn't been unhappy with my life necessarily, but she brought something more to it. It was like I had been living in black and white, and then after I met her, my entire world had been splashed with color. Everything was brighter and more vivid. Everything I saw, everything I heard, everything I *felt*, was somehow richer than before. It was definitely a very intense change, and it was all because of her.

And I wasn't going to let her fight this. Not anymore. I wasn't going to go back to black and white.

So, I said *fuck it*.

I decided that I had to touch more of her and I didn't want to refuse myself the pleasure of doing so.

I reached into her spandex pants and trailed my fingers down the lace thong she had on, going straight for her wet warmth. I ripped the lacy material aside and, without wasting any time, shoved two fingers deep inside her. I knew how close she was so there was no need to tease her. And the surprised gasp she let out when my fingers entered her was all the confirmation I needed that she not only liked it but wanted more of it.

She begged me not to stop, pleaded with me to keep going in her breathy voice. Which sent my blood rushing down south, increasing the size of the bulge in my shorts to a dangerous girth. She was writhing and riding my hand like her life depended on it. She was hot in my arms, and little did she know that nothing could have stopped me in that moment from giving her what she needed. Her walls started to clamp down, so I pumped even harder, desperate for her to taste that thrill.

"Yes, that's it. Come for me, baby."

At my words, she started to scream out her release before I brought my lips down onto hers, swallowing the rest of her sounds. As much as I craved to hear her scream my name as she took her pleasure, I also didn't want anyone to hear us and investigate the noises. She continued to moan and thrust her hips into me as she rode out the rest of her orgasm with my mouth fused to hers, her hands gripping my biceps and nails digging into my skin.

I absorbed everything she gave me. The way her head was thrown back, eyes closed, bottom lip sucked between her teeth, as she thrashed around in ecstasy. The sounds she made right before she plummeted over the edge. The feel of her core gripping my fingers and clenching down as they plunged her into that bliss.

She was tempting and bewitching. The most breathtaking siren I'd ever seen, let alone held, and I was irrevocably ensnared under her spell. I wanted to lose myself in her essence, to surround myself with her touch, her scent, her sounds. I just needed more of Gwen.

Eventually, her breathing steadied and I removed my hand, straightened her clothing for her, and gently lowered her to the ground. She opened her eyes to see me looking down at her with a grin on my face as I leaned in for a deep kiss. "You are so gorgeous. I want nothing more right now than to strip off your clothes and make you do that again."

Even though I just had two fingers deep inside her and she had come right in front of me, *because* of me, she still blushed at my statement. "Maybe it should be your turn instead," she said as her hand lowered, headed straight for my manhood.

I caught her wrist before she reached me. "I don't know if I could control myself right now if you touched me there. I'm a little on edge." *Actually, I'm pretty sure I might blow if she so much as looks at it right now.* I knew I needed to let her go and I was doing my best to calm down.

"I can help relieve some of that tension." I groaned at that and her eyes widened, like she was surprised by the boldness of her own words. I wanted to give in so bad and just let her do it. It wasn't like I'd last long at this point anyway. It was so hard to refuse her but I was barely holding on to the last ounce of my self-control.

"Oh, you have no idea how good that sounds, but I'm afraid a little just wouldn't be enough. I would want all of you, and I'm not going to take you for the first time in a park against a tree. This was just for you."

Actually, if she started it I would most assuredly finish it, park or not. I would strip her down in two seconds flat and bury myself so deep inside her, she'd feel me for the rest of the week. But I didn't want to say that, yet. I wasn't sure if she would still get easily spooked by my bluntness, so I thought it best left unsaid, at least until next time. Because there would absolutely be a next time. I'd make sure of it. And then I was going to do whatever the hell I wanted because I had a pretty good idea that Gwen would let me.

And she'd love it.

"Are you sure?" she asked, looking a little hurt, which made me feel like an asshole.

"I'm sure. You can make it up to me next time." I cupped her chin in one hand as I leaned down to give her a quick kiss on the lips and then stepped away from her. I couldn't have her touch me or I was seriously going to lose it.

"And when exactly will the next time be?" she asked, her nervousness evident in her voice.

"Soon. I promise," I assured her, stepping forward again and taking her hands in mine. "My schedule is going to be crazy for the next two weeks, but we'll figure it out, okay?"

She nodded her understanding, but her forehead creased in what looked like disappointment.

"Hey," I said softly, gently coaxing her to look me in the eyes. "We're going to have to be careful from here on out, but please don't ever doubt that I want this. No matter what happens, my feelings won't change. I hope yours don't either." I hoped my voice was conveying the sincerity of my words.

She shook her head as she stared up at me. "They won't. I may not be sure of how we're going to handle this, but I know how I feel and it's not going to go away." She paused and cast her eyes downward as she quietly said, "As long as *you* don't go away."

My chest tightened painfully at her words. She was afraid that I wasn't going to come back, that this would be it for us. That meant she wanted more of this. She wanted *us*.

That was all the confirmation I needed to know that we would somehow make this happen. We would figure it out. There was no other option.

I grinned down at her, taking her mouth in one last kiss and said, "I haven't wanted anyone or anything so much in my entire life, Gwen. I'm not going anywhere." Her shoulders immediately relaxed at what I said, and the most stunning smile I'd ever seen washed over her face. I had to pause for a moment to catch my breath at the sight. Satisfied that I had reassured her, I backed away from her, without losing eye contact, and said in a low voice, "Keep your phone on you. You'll be hearing from me soon." With that, I turned my back and walked back toward the main path.

Walking away from her and leaving her standing there, looking so vulnerable, was an insanely hard thing to do. But I had to for both our sakes. We had more time. Now that I had her and had convinced her that I wanted her, I was able to make more time with her. That took a minute to sink in, as I headed to my car.

I had Gwen now.

Not completely because she was still engaged, so we couldn't exactly go public, but I had her in some sense. Right now, I would take that.

No, I didn't like her going back to that bastard Callahan, but it would take some time to sort this situation out and convince her to leave him. I knew that their marriage was going to be a huge merging of both families, so I understood that it was going to be difficult to break it off, but it would happen. I would take however much time she needed to sort it all out, but one way or another she was going to end up with me. Because I was the right man for her. I was now certain of that.

But right now, I had a more pressing matter to attend to. Being that close to Gwen and not being able to have her like I want, yet, was really taking a toll on one particular body part. I had to find a cold shower to calm myself down. *Now*.

And if that didn't work, I could always try an ice bath.

CHAPTER FOURTEEN

OPPORTUNITIES AND DECISIONS

Gwen

Clay: *The Luxembourg. Tomorrow night. 8pm. Room 1109.*

That was the text I'd received over an hour ago and I hadn't yet responded. Clay wanted me to meet him alone at a hotel, at night, and William was going to be out of town tomorrow night. All night.

Oh, God. This is it. That moment when I've really got to decide how far I was going to take this. I felt like I'd been saying that a lot recently, but this was *really* it. This was us taking it far beyond anything and everything that had happened before and entering into a new realm of wrong. This meant *sex*, with Clay Masterson.

My heart started pounding in my chest, and I honestly didn't know if it was more from the fact that this was an extremely dangerous idea or from the possibility of having sex with Clay Masterson.

Can I go through with it, though?

That was *the* question I had to answer. And once I eventually sat down and contemplated it, I was both ecstatic and relieved that the fears and doubts that usually controlled my impulses weren't there anymore. That question didn't send me into a panic attack like it used to and like it almost had the other day in the park.

In fact, I was excited. Now, all I could think about was that I was going to finally have Clay all to myself and then I couldn't think of anything else. That man was going to be *mine* and suddenly I couldn't wait until tomorrow night. I'd get to see him naked. I'd get to touch him wherever I wanted. I'd get to hear all of the sexy noises he makes when I finally take him into my mouth.

Yep, it was definitely happening.

Me: *Tomorrow night. Can't wait.*

He responded not even ten seconds later.

Clay: *Good. Me either.*

I'd have to cancel girl's night even though I was really looking forward to it. *But you may never get this opportunity with Clay again.* That was true. As much as I hated to even think it, this may be the only chance we were ever going to have of being alone together with William gone, and I had a feeling that I would hate myself forever if I didn't take advantage of it.

I called Beatrice to cancel our plans with a promise to reschedule soon. What excuse was I going to give her for cancelling? Obviously, I couldn't tell her the truth. I could just blame it on my mother and say that she needed my help with some wedding planning stuff. It wouldn't be hard for them to believe that she would demand my presence, regardless of the plans I'd already made. It'd happened before, more than once.

She picked up on the second ring. "Hey, darlin'," she said in her heavy Southern drawl, "Twinkies or Ding Dongs tomorrow? One's chocolate so that's a winner already, but the other is a 'golden, yellow, delicious bastard,' to quote the wise Woody Harrelson." She sighed dramatically and added, "I'm torn."

I shook my head at her and smiled. Bea had a sweet tooth the size of Texas and she wasn't ashamed of it. All of the women I knew in this city would be absolutely appalled at the kind of stuff that she liked to scarf down, which I found hilarious and it forced me to love her even more. I just had no idea how in the world all of those calories didn't go straight to her hips. It was unnatural and almost disgusting how perfect she could look after going on a cream-filled snack cake binge.

"You and your sweets. You know one of these days you're going to go into a sugar coma, and I'm not going to be there to save you."

She scoffed and said, "You know what, I'm getting them both. It's not like one's healthier than the other, so I really shouldn't deny myself the pleasure of either."

My smile faded as I remembered the reason I'd called her in the first place. With talk of snack cakes and Woody Harrelson, I completely forgot what I needed to tell her.

"Actually," I began, "I'm going to have to cancel girl's night, Bea. My mother is demanding that I help her with some wedding stuff at their house tomorrow night."

She let out a gasp of outrage and I cringed. "No! She can't ruin girl's night! Can't you guys do that earlier in the day or somethin'?"

"Apparently not because she's got some function she has to go to in the afternoon. You know her." I made a face and felt so guilty that I was lying to my best friend. "I'm sorry. We can reschedule for next weekend, maybe?" I asked hopefully.

I really do need girl time and probably will more so after my night with Clay every-woman's-fantasy Masterson.

"And what am I supposed to do with all these snack cakes I just bought? And the five bottles of wine sittin' on my kitchen counter?"

I laughed. "Honey, you know you'll clean out the snack cakes in an hour. As for the wine, invite one of your boy toys over and take advantage of him. Isn't that your usual MO?" I teased.

She chuckled because she knew I was right. "I should resent that but I can't if it's true. You know me too well." She gave another dramatic sigh and said, "Fine. I'll save the wine for next weekend, but I'll probably have to buy more snacks, and you don't get to bail twice. Have fun with Mommy Dearest and hide the wire hangers."

I rolled my eyes but an image of my mother standing over me and screaming at me with a wire hanger in her hands flashed through my mind and my whole body shuddered. *Creepy.*

"Yeah, yeah. Tell Felicity I'm sorry and I love you both. We'll talk later."

"Ta-ta, love," she said in her best sophisticated, proper tone. She knew the other socialites thought her and Felicity's accents made them seem unrefined, so she liked to go overboard with the soft spoken lady routine when she was feeling particularly snarky.

I spent the rest of the day freaking out about Saturday night and writing material for the romance novel I had apparently decided to write. I was shocked at how effortlessly the words were coming to me. Ever since I met Clay, I had been more interested in writing about love and desire and passion, which had all been completely elusive concepts to me prior to that man stampeding through my life.

Of course, the danger in writing such stories—which was also most likely the reason I never wrote those types of stories to begin with—was that, at some point, your mind starts telling you that such happily ever afters are possible.

But I had to remember that I wasn't some heroine in a romance novel. I was just a closet romantic trapped in my dragon-guarded ivory tower and burdened by a loveless reality. And Clay might be a knight but he wasn't *my* knight.

Maybe my story never had one.

"I'll be busy the whole time I'm there, so I don't know if I'll have time to call before I get back," William said to me as he zipped his garment bag closed.

What that really meant was "I doubt I'll want to talk to you while I'm gone so don't expect a call." Well, that was fine with me.

Instead of saying that I just nodded and responded with, "I understand. You'll be busy. Don't worry about me."

It was ten o'clock on Saturday morning and he was about to leave to head into the office, thus beginning our weekend away from each other. I was counting down the hours, the minutes, until I would see Clay. But at the moment, I was more nervous about this goodbye with William. I had to make sure he didn't suspect anything before he left or the entire plan would be doomed.

He looked up and his eyes connected sharply with mine. "What are you going to do while I'm gone?"

Here we go. You have to be convincing.

I shrugged casually. "Probably just work on some wedding stuff with Mother and then stay home and watch some movies or read."

He searched my face for a minute longer, looking for any sign of deception. He was always paranoid like this, especially when he traveled out of town and left me here alone. I guess in this case, his paranoia was justified, though.

He was eventually satisfied and nodded. "I'll be at the office until five and then go straight to the airport from there. I'm supposed to get back in tomorrow night around eight." He lifted the garment bag off the bed and draped it over his arm as he started to walk out the bedroom door and down the stairs. "Call Rachel if you need something," he added dismissively.

"Okay," I said, following him down the stairs.

Roberto took William's bag from him at the front door and walked toward the waiting town car in the driveway.

William turned back to me with a hard, pointed look and in a low, severe voice said, "You'll be here waiting for me tomorrow night, then." He said it as a statement, not a question.

"Of course."

"Good." He grabbed my arm, yanking me towards him, and planted a harsh, possessive kiss on my lips, though it felt more like a brand. It was over quickly but my lips already felt bruised from the force of it.

With that, he walked out the front door and slid into the backseat of the car without a backwards glance.

My first task after William's car left the property was to catch my breath and calm my rapidly beating heart. My nerves were starting to get to me and doubt was starting to creep in. Agreeing to this was crazy, but I simply wasn't able to reject Clay or deny what he was doing to me.

The second task was to find out what in the world I was going to wear tonight. *What do you wear to a secret rendezvous with your would-be lover?*

Before Clay, I felt like my life was going nowhere fast. Everything was spinning out of my control and desperation for change had started to consume me. I was so tired of sacrificing my own happiness for others' satisfaction. Being with him made me want to throw all of that away. Every time I was around him, I had a staggering feeling that *he* was the change I was desperately seeking and I wanted to know more about him. *Had* to know more.

I was doing this for me because I wasn't yet willing to drive something, or someone, away and out of my life that could lead to something amazing. Most people would probably consider this wrong, immoral, or shameless, but if there was one thing that life had taught me, it was that things don't always happen the way you expect or plan for them to. Whatever curveballs life throws at you, you just have to adapt and deal with it the best possible way you know how.

The other thing that I'd learned recently, though, was that you also have to *live* your life the best way you know how. That was the part that I hadn't been doing so well, and I took full responsibility for it. This was my life, after all, and nobody could lead it but me. I've tended to place most of the blame for the direction my life has traveled on the people in my life that have influenced and controlled it: my parents and William. Although they had certainly played a part in making the decisions that led me to where I was at, I've still had the ultimate power to choose my path.

To surrender or to fight.

And up to this point, I'd chosen to surrender.

Well, not anymore. Now, it was time to fight. Fight for happiness. Fight for a different future. Fight for love? I wasn't sure if this was leading to that yet or not, but I felt like I might be on that precipice and I wanted to find out what was next.

I just hoped that I wasn't about to regret it.

Clay

Relax, she'll be here.

I knew she'd promised me that she would be, but I couldn't help feeling anxious. Anything could happen in this kind of situation. Callahan could have stopped her, her parents could have interfered somehow, or she could have just changed her mind and not bothered to call me.

She wouldn't do that, though. She wants to be here just as much as you do. I felt that in the park. I could see it in her eyes, hear it in her voice. She couldn't deny how her body reacted to me, but I knew it was also more than that. She didn't trust easily and I could tell that her mind was letting me in just as much as her body was.

I heard what my thoughts were telling me, but I still needed to calm down. So, I walked over to the small bar in the hotel suite and poured myself a couple fingers of bourbon. It wasn't the best stuff but it would do the trick. The liquid burned down my throat as I sat down in the leather chair near the window, letting the alcohol work its magic on my frayed nerves.

I never got this nervous over a woman, but this was Gwen. And this wasn't just some regular date with her, but tonight would be the turning point in our relationship. We both knew that. That was what had me freaking out. If it went poorly, I could very well lose my chance and altogether, lose her. That was not acceptable and I'd do my damnedest to make sure it didn't happen. She knew what this night meant, too, but the difference was, I wasn't sure what was going through her head. I knew she was sincere about what she'd said in the park, but she was still skittish and could easily change her mind about us.

That's what I'm here to fix. I wasn't going to leave this room until I was convinced that we were in this together. I couldn't keep second guessing myself about her feelings for me. I needed to be sure.

That was if she even showed up.

She was only ten minutes late, but it was D.C. and traffic in this part of town could always be rough. *Ten minutes doesn't mean anything.* I went over to the bed where I had left my phone just to make sure I hadn't missed a call or text from her but there was nothing. And I was starting to get anxious again. Apparently that bourbon only had short-term effects.

Another five minutes of pacing and scanning the streets below through the window, looking for any sign of her arrival, had me heading back to the bar for another drink. Just as I was about to pour, there was a soft knock on the door.

My heart stopped.

She came.

She was here.

Taking a deep breath, I walked over to the door and looked through the peephole to double check. Nobody else knew I was here but just to be safe.

There she stood. Her blonde hair was down around her shoulders in loose waves, she wore a black trench coat, and her head kept turning away to glance down the hallway, her bottom lip clenched between her teeth. She was nervous, too, and probably afraid of being seen.

I opened the door and was immediately assaulted by her delicious scent, the one I smelled day and night, whether she was anywhere near or not. A powerful surge of need swarmed through my body as I took in her face when she met my eyes. They were bright and alert but darkened slightly when she saw me, giving me a quick once over. I felt a bit of pride at her lustful gaze and had to control the burning temptation to yank her inside and take her against the door.

Although my eyes stayed on hers, I could tell she had her coat opened and her gorgeous legs were on display. I had all night to appreciate her body, though. Right now, I didn't want to break our gaze. I couldn't seem to find the right words in that moment, but I wanted to convey to her that things would change if she stepped inside this room. She wouldn't be able to just shut me out after tonight. She wouldn't be able to hide from me. She always seemed to be able to read my thoughts just by looking at me and I needed her to do that now. I needed her to know what I was saying without words because I wouldn't be able to go backwards if we took this next step together.

She seemed to understand what I was saying and didn't once waver from my stare. She straightened her shoulders and the corners of her lips started to curl up into a barely perceptible smile. There was the confidence. That was all the answer I needed.

"Hi, Gwen."

"Hey, Clay." Her voice was strong and not shaky in the least.

Good enough for me.

I stepped back and held the door open for her as she stepped inside.

I hoped she knew what she was in for because tonight I was going to take, savor, dominate, and devour.

And not necessarily in that order.

Tonight, Gwen McKindry was *mine*.

TO BE CONTINUED…

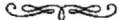

Stay tuned for *Possession and Politics: Part Two* coming August 2015!

Check out my Facebook page at facebook.com/melaniemuntonauthor for updates and teasers on my upcoming projects!

Send me an email at: melaniemuntonauthor@gmail.com

Also follow me on:

Twitter: @melanie_munton

Pinterest: pinterest.com/melaniemunton/

Instagram: instagram.com/melaniemunton/

A LETTER FROM THE AUTHOR

Dear Reader,

First and foremost, thank you so much for reading *Possession and Politics*! This is my first full-length novel, and it means the world to me that you were interested enough to learn more about these characters and their tumultuous journey. I'm so excited to share the rest of Gwen and Clay's story in Parts Two and Three which will be coming out soon (Part Two is due out August 2015)! I've loved developing their relationship and writing the dynamics of their situation and can't wait to reveal what their future holds!

This series is only the first in a long list of others that I have planned in the near future, beginning with the first of the three-part *Cruz Brothers* serials, a spin-off of *Possession and Politics*, set to release late 2015/early 2016. The series will follow Parker from *P & P*, along with his brothers, Mason and Dawson, and how they struggle with facing the demons of their past in order to fight for the relationships they don't want to lose. I'll also be releasing the first of the four-part (possibly more!) *For Love* series around the same time, which will follow the journeys of four different couples. Their stories are intense, crazy, heartwarming, heart wrenching, suspenseful and altogether, just plain *steamy*. But don't worry, I'm not always serious! I've got some romantic comedies up my sleeve that I absolutely cannot wait to share with the world. So, if you like dry humor with sarcastic, slightly neurotic and oftentimes accident-prone female leads, you do NOT want to miss these!

Again, thank you so very much for reading *Possessive and Politics*, and if you liked Gwen and Clay's story, go like my Facebook page (don't forget to share it with your other book-collecting, reading-obsessed friends) and tell me about it! I'd love to hear your feedback, so feel free to post on my wall or email me at melaniemuntonauthor@gmail.com. And if you're feeling particularly verbose, I would be so grateful if you'd be willing to leave a review on the platform through which you purchased this book. It would sure put a smile on my face. ☺

I hope this book has certainly piqued your interest and you're as anxious for the release of *Possession and Politics: Part Two* as I am! Remember to follow my Facebook page because that is where all of my updates, teasers and other project details will be posted until I can get my website up and running (I don't know about you, but I'm no expert in coding and website design so it's been a learning process).

Thanks for giving me and my book a chance. You have no idea how much I appreciate it. I hope you're going to stick around for the future because it's going to be one hell of a crazy ride!

All my love,

Melanie

Like my page and follow me on Facebook at www.facebook.com/melaniemuntonauthor!

ACKNOWLEDGEMENTS

To my husband, Sean, my pioneer, my champion, my rock. You've always believed that I could do this and you never stopped encouraging me. Ever since we met you've been my biggest supporter, and I absolutely could not have done this without you by my side, picking me up when I'm down and always knowing how to lift my spirits. I can't thank you enough for your endless patience with me whenever I get lost in my world of fiction or whenever I let my frustrations (and sassiness) get the better of me. I don't deserve the love and understanding you show me every day, but I thank God for every minute that I have with you. I'm so grateful that He's put you in my life and given me the greatest love I could ever know. I'll never be able to express to you in words how you've affected my life. It may not always seem like it, but you make me a better person and have since the day I met you. You've given me the ability to write about love and to know what it's like to surrender your heart and soul to another person. You've made me the happiest woman in the world, which also makes me the luckiest woman in the world. You're the light of my life, my smile on a gloomy day, my sunshine above the clouds, my end and my beginning. There's no one else in the world that I'd want to live out my days with, and I can't wait to see what else life has in store for us.

To my parents, Tim and Sherri, I am who I am today because you gave me a foundation on which to build a life full of love, happiness, and faith. No other parents could have shown more love and support than you have for my entire life, and I will forever thank you for that. You taught me how to be a strong individual and to pursue every goal and chase every dream that I've had. Knowing that I've had both of you to catch me if I fall means more to me than you will ever know. Over the years, you've instilled in me a sense of determination to reach far beyond what I thought I was capable of and achieve more than I ever imagined I could. Thank you for loving me through all of the stress, worry, and frustration I'm sure I've put you through over the years. I honestly couldn't have better parents.

To my grandparents, I wouldn't have even half of the amazing experiences that I have without your help, love and support over the years. You've been remarkably understanding and generous my whole life, oftentimes when I didn't even deserve it. You've done more for me and continue to do more for me than a grandchild, or any person for that matter, has any right to hope for. I am constantly amazed by your unwavering compassion and boundless love, and you are all truly some of the most kindhearted people I will ever meet. I am so proud to call you my grandparents and to be your Miss Priss.

To my brother, Tymon, and his wife, Kim, what can I say but I love you two? You two have always encouraged me in all of my endeavors, without judgment, and I cannot tell you what your support has meant to me. I know you guys will always be there if I need you, without question, which was actually one of the things that gave me the courage to pursue this dream in the first place. You guys know my crazy, my angry, my attempts to be funny, and my happy...and you still love me anyway (at least I hope you do). Tymon, even though we can fight 'til the cows come home, you always know where I'm coming from and respect my opinion and individuality (even if you don't admit it). Kim, you've added a lightheartedness to our family that I think we desperately needed, and you've given me some of the best memories of my life (Blondes with Backpacks is on the horizon!), so thank you for those. I seriously cannot wait for our families to expand (love you, Oliver!) and for all of the future memories we will share together.

To my other brother, Taylor, don't think I forgot about you, dude. I know that I was frustrating to have as an older sister when we were kids, but I love the relationship that we've formed as we've both grown up. We can talk and laugh about some of the stupidest things but still have serious discussions about life and I'm so thankful for that. I look at you now as a friend, and not just as my little brother, and I know that no matter what, you'll always have my back. You're hilarious and fun to be around, and you have one of the biggest hearts of anyone I know. You've influenced more of my story ideas and characters than you probably realize and I thank you for that. I look forward to watching you grow as a person and I can't wait for future family vacations. I love you and your long hair (go for the man bun!).

To Barbara, I don't even know what to say. You've been my confidant through this, you've been my encouragement, and you were my first ever beta tester/editor! Your notes and suggestions were a tremendous help, and seeing as how you were my first reader, your honesty was a huge relief to me. You've listened to me vent about anything and everything countless times over the years, and I can't thank you enough. When I wanted to share my new venture with someone, you were there to offer friendship and support when I needed it and you understood exactly where I was coming from. Your advice has been priceless to me, and I can't tell you what it's meant to me to have you involved in this process before anybody else was. You're one of the few people that I will always keep close to my heart and I value our friendship more than words can express. Woof!

To all of my other family and friends from Cabool to Carthage, from Springfield to St. James to Steelville and everywhere else in between, thank you all so much for your love and support throughout the years. You've all been a huge inspiration to me and this journey I'm now embarking on and you continue to be as I move forward. The memories you've all given me will always serve as a reminder of what an amazing support system I have and the fact that I have some of the best people in the world in my corner. I love every single one of you and wish I could see you guys every day.

To Alisha at Damonza, thank you so much for working with me on the cover designs! Thank you for bringing the pictures in my head to life and for being spectacularly awesome throughout the entire process. You're pretty much amazing and I look forward to future covers.

Last but certainly not least, I have to thank all of my readers. To everyone who went out and purchased this book, whether you know me personally or you just saw the blurb online and thought it sounded like a good read, THANK YOU SO FREAKING MUCH! It really is a fantastic feeling to know that I have people out there reading my work, and I want nothing more than for you to love it and want to come back for more. I'm putting so much work into this series, as well as future projects, and I hope that you'll stay with me as I share these worlds and the lives of the characters that I love so much with you. It's sure to be a scary, crazy and sometimes stressful trip, but I know that continuing to have your support as a reader will be all of the motivation I need to give each and every story all that I've got! You guys are amazing, and if I could, I would hug and kiss all of you!

ABOUT THE AUTHOR

Melanie Munton is an up-and-coming romance author who favors contemporary romance, romantic suspense, and romantic comedies above all others. She loves writing stories about characters who struggle to rise above the obstacles that plague them but who eventually find their victory and salvation in the person they fall in love with. *Possession and Politics* is her first full-length novel trilogy, and she will introduce two new series, the *Cruz Brothers* serials and the *For Love* chronicles, beginning late 2015/early 2016.

Melanie was born and raised in a small rural town in the heart of the Missouri Ozarks. She earned her degree in Anthropology from Missouri State University, where she met her husband, Sean. Four years and a semester abroad later, they married in a beautiful outdoor ceremony near her hometown. They decided to make a fresh start and moved to North Carolina in late 2014, where she realized her passion for writing. Although she had always been a fan of any and all fiction (she comes from a family full of readers), especially romance, she finally decided to write down all the stories that had been floating around in her head, thus beginning her writing career. Now, she writes during the day from their modest two-bedroom townhome and takes weekend trips to the beach with her husband as often as she can.

One of Melanie's favorite things to do is travel with her husband. She backpacked Western Europe and spent a semester studying abroad in Spain during her college years and can't wait to go back. Melanie and Sean love to go on road trips together and have an entire list of archaeological sites all over the world that they plan on visiting throughout their lives.

Not only does Melanie hail from a family of readers, but also from a family of movie-watchers. Playing movie trivia games, among other types of board games, with her family is one of her all-time favorite things to do. It's no secret that the Bays take their games seriously, so things tend to get pretty heated but they always love each other in the end. Melanie also has one of the most eclectic tastes in music of anyone you've ever met and will listen to almost anything from Van Halen to The Temptations, from hip-hop and R&B to New Age, from Classical to Celtic instrumental. You name it, she'll listen to it, and she loves to incorporate all types of music into her stories. Along with music, one of her (and her entire family's) favorite activities to do is dance, and she's convinced that with enough encouragement and coaxing she'll eventually transform her unwilling, no-rhythm-having husband into Lord of the Dance and is, in fact, making it one of her life goals.

Melanie has a horrible addiction to pasta and could eat it for every meal if she wasn't worried about the carbs. She considers cream soda to be the most delicious beverage ever put on this earth, and you can guarantee that she always has some sort of candy with her. Whether it's Sprees, Nerds, Hot Tamales, or all forms of chocolate, she most assuredly has a bag of it and has threatened the lives of those who have gotten too close to her stash, even her husband.

Above all else, she cherishes her relationships with all of her family, friends, and God. She lives for the precious moments when she gets to see all of them and wishes everyone could get together more often. Right now, however, she's absolutely exuberant about the new writing path she's traveling down and can't wait to see what the future holds for her!